Friends And Occasional Lovers

Diane M Kent

Also by Gillman Noonan
and published by Poolbeg Press

A Sexual Relationship and other stories

Friends And Occasional Lovers

GILLMAN NOONAN

poolbeg press

First published 1982 by
Poolbeg Press Ltd.,
Knocksedan House,
Swords, Co. Dublin, Ireland.

Cover by Robert Ballagh based on a screen painted by
the artist and in the collection of Gordon Lambert.

Some of these stories first appeared in "The
Irish Press" *New Irish Writing*.

Printed by Cahill Printers Limited.
East Wall Road, Dublin 3.

Contents

Gillman Noonan was born in Kanturk, Co. Cork, studied at U.C.C., and worked in various parts of Europe, particularly Germany and Switzerland. His first short story was published in The Irish Press "New Irish Writing" page in 1973 and he won the Writers' Week in Listowel Short Story Award in 1975. His first collection of stories, "A Sexual Relationship", was published by Poolbeg Press in 1976.

Jealousy

Under the green quilt, dark blue in the curtained light, Pascal lay trapped, a creature in hot sand, tongue unsticking, the eyes still gummed in their sockets. Judy's breathing was free, a winged miracle drifting with the dip and rise of the desert. Myles, his body aflame in the sun, was circling her with easy grace. 'What lovers we have!' cried Pascal angrily, struggling to follow. But it was only numbness and the last coils of dream which he shook off, turning over and lifting the dead tingling arm as if it were a stump. Judy turned with him but slept on, her face hidden in the crook of her arm.

Pascal flexed his fingers until life returned to them, stretched and breathed deeply. The feeling of weight persisted and he wondered about it as if it were a new and unexpected symptom of his disorder. For weeks, especially on waking, he had been assailed rather by the fragility of it all. Walls of rooms were boxes wafer thin, the car would crumple around him like foil, Judy's skin would come away at his touch. It was so close to him now when he turned his head that the faint down on her arm stirred in his breath. It quickened him. The ovals of scar tissue looked tender yet deep and porous and, guiltily, as if robbing a drop of some sweet promise her body secreted, he touched them with his dry lips. Her breathing stopped, set in again slow and even but this time he sensed that she was awake and willing him to leave the bed. He lay on for a while pondering the justice of it, for in the small hours, annoyed that she hadn't rung, he too had feigned sleep.

He shaved and dressed. On the landing he stood a moment and listened. How still the house was. The girls were away at summer camp. He missed them. They were soft and silly and his. Opening the door of Don's room he looked in. The boy was awake and they talked about the tennis tournament. Posters of tennis stars covered the walls and Pascal delayed, pretending to study them, savouring the quiet father-son intimacy but its frailty too, for Don was Judy's blood, the same cat-like reserve in the fine bones, eyes and mouth impatient as if to say, *Well, what else*? She would applaud his winning strokes, comfort him if he lost, and later they might recount some of the happenings to Pascal but only as part of their pleasure at reliving them together.

'Remember,' he said at the door, 'the bigger they come . . .'

'I know,' said the boy turning his head away. *Go. Go.*

Pascal thought of mother and son as partners in an intricate dance to which he was occasionally admitted but as a gauche bumpkin unsure of the steps. Plugging in the kettle he wished again that the girls were there to scamper about and jeer. It was normal, he reflected, holding bread and teacup and wandering into the front room. All families had their camps. And as if demanding a printout of normality he scanned years, outings, sickness, Eileen framed there in her First Communion dress, the shrubs outside they had planted together.

The sun filtering through the lace curtains mocked him, an ailing sun feeding even now before day had rightly begun on its own light, sucking from the objects and photographs their mass and colour, draining *him* of life so that the cup hung heavy on his finger and the bread turned to ashes. And for a moment the panic returned

— house, street, shell, set, mantelpiece a painted board, shrubs cut-outs, children allies summoned to the still place where he and Judy stood alone. He saw Myles and Judy throwing weeds at each other in the stream beside the forge but instead of weeds it was this family bible of memory. Leaves fell from it, fluttered down into the water and floated past his legs. Myles and Judy laughed. The children laughed. And why not? Weren't they dead things? What bible was a match for the ardent now?

Or what was he imagining? Brenda stood at the cottage door, a small ragamuffin bursting with child. Did she suspect? And even if she did, would she care? They were bohemian. Debts? She laughed at them. And laughed too, touching her forehead to Pascal, at Myles and Judy, the young cousins who had found each other after years. What children they were, arguing. *What lovers we have*, he had cried in his dream.

'Lovers how are you,' he said now, slurping his tea, but the sneer betrayed uncertainty, and obeisance almost as one said Little People to appease the demon one feared. And, eyeing the clock, knowing near to the minute when he could still slip through the bottlenecks of traffic, he tarried as if determined (gazing out at the shrubs) to fit the scene back into its original 'normal' frame: the rickety old table set up on the bank for tea, children splashing, Myles stripped to the waist slashing at weeds, all of them, Myles, Brenda, Judy and himself loud in argument over what? yes, competition and why there must be such or so much ('Like weeds!' Brenda shouted) in the world. It was all right for Myles, he had argued, making his rustic Irish furniture, choosing his clients. He didn't have to run a factory in the rag trade in the middle of a recession. 'Poor Pascal! Poor Pascal!' Myles had smiled at him. He understood perfectly of course. And Pascal understood too, watching them throwing weeds, Judy pursued into the forge, that the shape rather than the content of ideas was the game, and he was too straight and factual (humour-less?) to be part of it. But the picture he took with him into the traffic—as he knew he would, as if whatever framing he contrived it would focus before he left the house—was Myles' pale body emerging from the dark workshop where the blacksmith had toiled followed by Judy flushed and smiling as at some secret only they would share.

'Morning, Pascal.'
'Morning, Jimmy.'
'Looking glum?'
'Monday blues.'

Was it that evident? He forced himself to smile, won-dering then as he threw himself into a flurry of work how great the change in him had appeared to others. He had become moody, often forgetful (as now, seeing the Ger-man buyer waiting for him, he had quite forgotten that he was expected). Pascal losing his edge? He strode forward, hand outstretched.

'Guten tag, Herr Kunze!'
'Guten tag, Herr Ward!'

'But that's as far as we'll go in your language,' said Pascal, and the two men laughed. This was the first consignment of raincoats for Kunze's stores in the Rhine-land and he had come over specially to check them out. His reputation as a buyer was at stake. Now that the big chains were not coming through with the orders as they used to, Noleen Ltd. was cultivating the smaller outlets — too late perhaps, the company was in trouble. And Kunze had his standards. Sleeves must hang at the right angle, seams must be unpuckered. Even in the lower price range a raincoat was a fashion garment for the German woman. 'Fit and finish,' he liked to say, unaware that he had already been given that nickname in the office.

Girls were summoned to the display room to try on

samples. They stood blushing under the German's expert eye and small soft hands touching now the waist, now the shoulders, ocasionally slipping along the lapel and lightly over the bust. It was close. Hovering in the background Pascal felt the need to belch but coudn't.

'Lunch around half-twelve, Herr Kunze?'

'Fine, Mr. Ward.'

On the factory floor the ryhthms of the day were setting in and Pascal, throwing off his jacket, opened his senses to the noise and movement. Activity was a drug and he sucked it in greedily. But of late while he listened and nodded or talked and pointed he was aware of his need and thus perversely immune to it. Much as a drinking man gauges his intake and the level of his response, his mind remained inert, locked in upon itself.

Two men were hanging up a large sign over the lines: STOP THINK SAFETY FIRST. Collins the supervisor was standing beside one of the machines, waiting for the electrician. Perhaps all that was needed was to tighten a screw but he couldn't do it. Pascal pulled a face in passing and Collins smiled. Several times before the week was out the same kind of signal would pass between them, part resignation, part complicity in a higher understanding. Mrs. Duff beckoned, introduced him to a new girl and for a while he watched her manipulate the matrix on her first batch of collars. It was easy enough and she glanced up at him, pleased with herself.

Pascal looked at the clock. Soon they would be leaving for the tournament. Would she call to the forge on the way home? Brenda was in hospital having her baby. Could Myles cook?

Dry in the mouth, bilious, Pascal sat in his glass cubicle overlooking the production area. STOP THINK the sign admonished in huge scarlet letters, the rest hidden from his view by the lamps. On a dummy in the corner someone had painted a funny face meant to be his, the quiff and moustache exaggerated to make him look like Hitler. To his right girls were giving coats a final brush down, moving them along the hangers. All day long brushing, brushing, but they talked and laughed and joined in snatches of the musak. And there was the short vibrant figure of Kunze again with Mrs. Duff fussing at his elbow. They were checking lists, batches.

Pascal was gripped by the sensation that everyone down there was alive and he was dead, a ghost of himself revisiting his old office, sitting with the dictaphone to his lips but no thoughts forming, not a word spinning onto the tape, the world beyond rushing by like wind through a tunnel. A premonition of when the place would close its doors? Perhaps he should move now, quickly, this month. There was that job with Celtic Carpets. Or even LPR sacks . . .

Ten thirty.

Usually he found some excuse to ring home at about eleven. He felt cheated though he sensed that she had come to dread it, his voice, the patent flimsiness of the pretext. He was wooing her but awkwardly and she, curled beside the fire, blinked at him or brightly parried with the foil of her intellect. The other night he had wanted to hit her. Instead, he said, 'Want to go to the theatre next week, Judy? There's that play by . . .' 'You don't like the theatre.' 'But *you* do.' 'So you'd be going for me.' 'Yes.' 'Wouldn't that be rather silly?' 'Why, if it gives me pleasure?' 'But would it?' And the sex was the same, brisk, not unloving but efficient, rather like dictating a familiar letter, here a change of emphasis, there an exclamation mark where there had been none. Once he had phoned from a bar in Munich and she had been vague, distracted, and afterwards in the company of a sparkling young whore he had lapsed, sentimental and a bit drunk. When he had tried to tell her about it (why? seeking some confrontation that might purify?) she had quickly placed her hand over his mouth and shaken her head, and in bed later she had opened to him warm and giving with surges of the old wild bronco passion mottling her face and neck, smiling down at him then in the calm as though wordlessly to convey that never would anything of the sort matter between them. But had he given *her* a right or had she, cleverly, taken one?

The new girl bent over her machine. He saw Judy taking up the hem of Eileen's Communion dress. *Keep still.* Pins clamped between her lips, hair awry, toothless old woman, her girl's neck. All of them, girls on his left, Don on her right, kneeling at Mass. What of their religion? No more than the other family bible would it be an obstacle. It was an unrisen cake, moist and indigestible at the core but dutifully garnished, a few angels, a little hell, for the children. Myles never much thought of God, he said, his long brown hand stroking the edge of a table as if it were an instrument.

STOP THINK.

Ten forty. *He couldn't work.*

'Dear Dummy,' he mentally dictated, holding up a fistful of papers and swivelling on his chair. 'Don't be such an ass. You're dreaming it all up. Do you know what jealousy is? It's a poison that you wouldn't wish on your worst enemy. Everything she does, everything they do together is magnified out of all proportion and it eats into you, devours you, my friend, like a cancer. Like last night pacing the floor wanting to phone her parents to find out if she was really there. You're behaving like a typical jealous middle-aged man with a young wife. What happens in marriage is . . .'

A secretary placed some documents on the table and he dictated aloud, 'With this in mind and in view of the present shortfall in the supply of . . . Thanks, Mary . . . in the supply of . . .'

What happens, he thought, dictating now at a furious

rate as if his Critical Path Analysis had at last revealed itself, is that a young girl from a brilliant loveless family, craving ordinary human contact and affection, meets a fine mature (and rather lonely) man who gives her all in his store of that commodity because he falls for her in a big way, and together they fall into the back of his car where she immediately conceives. However, they marry and become a real dandy family.

She begins to visit her brilliant loveless parents again as if to discover what she had fled from, what kind of love was denied her, and she finds them to be isolated people too aware of themselves, sceptical of all happiness. And she changes, often at the breakfast table looking pensive as if wondering how she had got there and who was this man in his pinstripe suit with whom she was sharing her life. Was she discovering the lie of love, the guile of its salvation? Should he have been merely a haven for her first turbulent flight? Perhaps she realises as time passes how much more her parent's child she is after all, diffident, remote, than his loving wife. But her apartness, the subtle retreat into her maturing self, is lost in the stir of family life, in the alibis of camps—he in league with the girls, she with the boy—in parental visits and outings and sickness and Communion dresses and all the rest. They are a family . . .

Until someone like cousin Myles comes on the scene with his lips rich and dark as ripe sloes, his curtained eyes and long brown hands that can finger the bars of a country 'fool's chair' as they would the strings of a harp, his sense of innocence and unentanglement in the alibis of his or any other family . . . and suddenly as if veils had been ripped aside and all thrown into high relief, there she is, a young woman still and one that appears reborn, her eyes sparkling, her soul flowering in this man's presence, a *woman* plain and simple with none of her appetites diminished . . . But Dummy there doesn't see it that way because in fact he hasn't changed much at all, he's like railway tracks that only cross other tracks to continue in other straight lines. And worse, He realises that he still sees her as that fledgling girl who lay trembling and unprotected in his arms. He would save her *again* from the big bad wolf . . .

STOP THINK.

Grow up, Pascal told his silly effigy. Let her off and have her fun and talk, it's all innocent anyway. Stop your phoning and wooing. What a ridiculous word, a lovesick owl woo-ooing in the trees!

A moment later, sipping a cup of coffee, he was thinking that he *could* however ring the forge. Perhaps the baby had arrived. How was Myles managing with the children? When would be the earliest she would get there?

The phone rang. It was Judy.

'Yes, Judy?' His heart missed a beat. 'Anything wrong?'

'No, no, I just wanted to remind you of the ad for the kittens. You won't forget, will you?'

'Okay. Calling to the forge on your way home?'

'May do. Why?'

'Oh I was just wondering if the baby had arrived.' He added, recklessly, 'It occurred to me that Myles probably can't cook an egg. Perhaps you should stay the night and at least see that they're fed.'

'Perhaps I will at that.' She sounded amused. 'You'll be all right?'

'No, the Little People will run off with me . . . Good luck to Don again.'

Sick, triumphant, he replaced the receiver.

It was a pyrrhic victory and he knew it. Over lunch with Herr Kunze a small mean voice set in, the Dummy's, he was convinced, getting his own back, urged on by a bunch of disgruntled Little People. What will she wear? it asked. She rang from the club and will hardly go back home again since the forge is practically on her way.

Brenda's things are too small. Would she wear a pair of his pyjamas? But he probably doesn't wear any. Where will she, they, sleep?

'What do you think of the Nanz group's performance?' he asked Kunze, stumbling back into the conversation.

Later, over cream liqueurs, Kunze talked of his pipes which filled an entire wall at home and of which he smoked but one, if at all possible, every twenty-four hours. And thence to Kunze's wife (from the photo a homely looking person in a white furry cap) whom he, Kunze, had finally convinced of the value of transcendental meditation. Pascal, his stomach a peculiar mixture of lead and bubbles, saw Kunze as an ideal pipe and his wife as an ideal pipe cleaner employed once, if at all possible, but then thoroughly, every twenty-four hours. He was informed of the square metreage of the Kunze flat (including balcony and cellar), the original, present and foreseeable price of the square metre. Indelibly, with the assurance of a trim balding school teacher showing how it worked, Herr Kunze imprinted himself on the world scene.

Alone, picking his way down through the crowds of Grafton Street to place the advertisement, Pascal stopped suddenly as if remembering something, stood looking in a shop window and thought: I've lost faith. That's what it is. It has nothing to do with jealousy. *I'm on the run.* He had a vision of himself as a cypher, a policeman of blind energies, and it was immaterial what these produced, raincoats or carpets or heavy duty sacks. At the same time he saw Myles bending over a·table and fussing with it, disappearing into the wood like a genie. Was *that* the real seat of his jealousy?

Someone put the question through the computer and on the VDU screen appeared the words COMMAND INVALID.

'Idiot,' he muttered, walking on. 'Of course it is. I'm a manager. I must be able to manage anything.'

When he had filled out the form he waited in line. She had remembered the kittens, he thought with satisfaction. Their kittens, in their garage. He saw them in their battered cardboard crib waiting for a home. And he would find them one. He, Pascal Ward, would manage that too. His tall frame loomed rich and important behind a frail grubby man with shaky hands. On the wall the fractional seconds of a digital clock squirmed, an ecstatic worm of time. Pascal kept his eyes on the young girl behind the counter.

She looked fresh and efficient and thoroughly reliable.

Haiku and High Octane

I am putting this down to be read only when I'm gone. It will be part of my literary estate.

Hannah May went over the cliff down by Deasy's corner and the sergeant came to call. He's straight out of fiction, four daughters and a cow. The big black boots proceeded over to where I lay under Hogan's old pick-up wrestling with the exhaust.

'Hallo there, Michael.'

'Hallo there, sergeant.'

'Fine day.'

'Thank God.'

I poked my head out and gave him a grin but decided to remain on my back tinkering away. I have found that you can never tell a man's expression when he's upside down. The mother and myself would live in great harmony if we could hang from everything by our toes.

After some chat the sergeant said, 'Sad thing that about Hannah May.'

'Very sad,' I said. Tinker, tinker. 'She must have had a drop in.'

'Aye.' The sergeant mopped his pate. He's bald like myself but we call him Bald Tyres because that had been his official fetish when he first came to the neighbourhood. No other county prosecuted so many bald tyres.

The lace over the kitchen window moved. She was peeping. The tea would be drawing and a plate of biscuits

18

on the table. The sergeant and herself had crept out of the same bog and between tea and whiskey and biscuits she couldn't do enough for him. Of course she had a vested interest too because he helped her farm out her greyhounds and kept his big red ear close to the ground. Also she hadn't given up hope of hitching me to the last of the daughters, Joanie. A nice girl and the right height for me too, four foot nine, but that's about all, I think .

'You were in Hogan's on Saturday night?'

I was, as always, though this time I had Bessie along. I was taking her to Ryan's dog. We never made it. The more heat John Barleycorn pumped into my veins the less I was inclined to believe that Bessie was in any. When I let her off the lead on the way home and magniloquently told her to have it away where she pleased she only wagged her tail at me. Now the sergeant couldn't have known this but he knew everything else, down to what tourists had been in the pub.

'And you didn't see Hannah May all evening?'

'Not a glimpse,' I lied. 'The poor woman.'

'Will you have a drop of tea, Joe?' said herself from the door. With her new dentures in and a fresh apron. Oh a brave little match-maker.

I had a sense of *deja vu,* if you'll forgive me. The setting sun, the sergeant stooping through the kitchen door, my skin sticky and alive with rust and muck. On the Saturday evening he had called just like this, though it had rained. He was tipping me off about a stolen Cortina but before the squad car appeared I had been lying like a man in a daze looking at an oily puddle beside my nose. I have a local reputation for going into trances. It's because I'm a bit of a poet, you see. I send in poems to the local paper and sometimes I get one published. But people never think of that when they see me in a trance. They only think I'm a bit touched, which of course is true too.

It was a special evening, that Saturday, and that's why

I can remember every detail of it. There was herself getting ready for confession and bingo. There was myself staring at the puddle utterly gripped by the *idea* of colour and by the thought that thirty-three years ago that day I had popped out of herself screaming *into* colour. But so far there hadn't been a word about 'the day that's in it.' That's all she ever said, and I never said a word about her birthday because I didn't even know when it was. I suppose it was natural enough for her to know when mine was. But 'the day that's in it' would mean that the moment had come to slide a few notes over the table beside my usual weekly rake-off. A couple of years back it was two, then with inflation it increased to three and four and I was making bets with myself that this year it would be a round fiver. By God, I was thinking of nipping over to the casino.

In came Bald Tyres anyway to tell me about the Cortina (and as far as I was concerned they could steal the whole damn lot of them) and where should his big clodhopping boot come down but into the lovely slinky shimmering colours on my puddle. But within minutes while he was away having his tea with herself and I was drifting back into another trance I realised that it was a fine haiku moment. I'm sold on haiku. When I came upon a book of them a few months ago I knew at once that this was the discipline I needed because my poetry was tending to be too *un*disciplined. I had been going through a bad period where I couldn't see a ditch for a ditch without ferreting around it for universals (On Falling into the Universal Ditch)—or I'd start off saying something nice and simple about a person and end up with three thousand million lunatics looking for an author. The haiku is your man for discipline. In its seventeen syllables (if you want to be purist) I found release. But even more than the formal discipline which abounds in all kinds of verse I had to rinse the old psyche of conflict before I got a word down because conflict *precedes* the haiku. It's all over bar the image which is resolved, total, living in its own associations and radiance. Bald Tyres' boot hitting the colours beside my eyes was enough. It didn't matter a hoot to me what the man did in his spare time, whether he sucked his tea like a mudfish or even finally roped me into the corral with his rolypoly daughter.

The sergeant's black boots

I can hit that first five-syllable line no bother. Naturally it was all wrong because nothing in the four words suggested that the boots were six inches from my nose. I would have to work on it and it didn't worry me that I would probably never achieve it. The great Japanese master, Basho, said a man could consider himself lucky to capture nine or ten real haiku moments in his lifetime. I know what he means because I haven't captured one fully satisfying one yet. Of course the Japs have the right approach because for them life, art and mental attitudes are one—or at least your poet aims at making them one whereas we are very wary of that kind of thing. We think it smacks of bohemianism. You might laugh at me there under my pick-up worrying about being bohemian but if you do you've missed the point—as anyone in the neighbourhood would tell me go see the bonesetter if I remarked that I was finding it difficult getting the hackles out of my haiku. Now Basho could ramble into a pub for his scoop of saki and say words to the same effect and all the old fellows sitting around would know exactly what he meant. Maybe the words were wrong but equally well the *mental attitude* might be wrong and they would understand that in a different way to us.

I occasionally come close even when herself, a diabolically disruptive force, comes into the picture. The other day I saw her taking in the washing and there it was: snap-click went the old eye's shutter:

My socks on the line
Full of the sun and dancing.
By her black arms plucked.
It's still full of aggro, isn't it?

To get on with it anyway, there I was with her when Bald Tyres had left having my own tea while she got ready for her confession and bingo. The teeth were back in their glass again. I never saw teeth migrate so fast. If they took wing and flew off to a warmer clime I wouldn't have been surprised.

Pieces of gristle
In small even teeth squirming.
A hare ripped open.
Get out the hara-kiri set.

The Good Shepherd watched me from over the fire. By the dresser was a wedding photograph. Dada slight and trim in his dark-blue suit. Herself a shy young girl of seventeen with her bunch of flowers. If only Dada had lived and Eileen, or if Tom hadn't gone to America or even if Mary had married in the parish. All the ifs. But we were alone, the two of us, touching the same things, full of the same smells and noises, sharing the night sounds of beam and bat, mouse and dog, the ocean's murmur. But untouchables, experts now at our own semaphore of grudging co-existence.

In she came in her egg-yoke slip, drying her face. I had once pulled at those dugs. From those grey eyes had sucked too. Her hand had rested warm and soft upon me. On the old wind-up gramophone she had attempted, amid laughter, to yank me into the secrets of the Cuckoo Waltz. Once in a flickering kitchen, in the tick-tock silence, she said to me, and I believed her; 'Prayer, sonny, is the noblest thing we have.'

All soured, soured utterly. I had become a sceptic, an anarchist behind mossy walls, in her eyes doomed already. I hadn't really wanted to. The lure of salvation is strong. But one morning doubt slipped under my skin like a jungle creature and nested there mingling its bright venom with my own. Perhaps it was just between the two of us and God had no part in it. Perhaps I only resented her prayers for me—and she pleaded my case daily—in my rejection of the reverence she had tried to instill into me for Pull, for manipulating the local Good Shepherds. I couldn't look at the one over the fire now without seeing Omar Sharif with a stiff neck from posing, anxious to get off the set to a stiff whiskey away from the phoney sheep. And her expression was one I had come to expect on Saturday nights, tense, expectant, her mind fixed somewhere between the dancing balls of the bingo machine and Omar's silky voice in the church telling her he would talk to the Boss but she must be patient.

The big moment. Scoured, dentured, scarfed, eau-de-cologned, costumed, an epileptic fag between her lips, she slipped a few notes across to me and then (pay the man) the fiver.

'For the day that's in it.' I mumbled my thanks. I always had. What a fine anarchist I was. At the door she said, 'Joanie says there's a good band at the hop. Are ye going?'

'I don't know,' I said, staring at the crisp new fiver.

'But you'll take Bessie down first, will you?'

I sat looking at the kitchen. It was like any ordinary Saturday night. I would wash, change, head for the village. Yet I couldn't move, trapped by a sense of doom. The kitchen was a stage set for a peasant play with its oilcloth on the table, its dresser of speckled delft, even a pail of soft well water (we liked to drink it) in a cool corner. The light had faded into a theatrical sky, lurid. Beyond the point the drowned sun still bled, seeping up into the dirty clouds. Any moment now someone would come through the door and say a few words and the play would unfold. But no one came. It had been conceived

staged, illuminated and, on a whim, abandoned. I sat
bewitched. Looking at the Good Shepherd I felt a certain
sympathy for him. How easy it was to be bewitched!
What magnificent sets!

I doodled:

> *God is a graphic designer*
> *Who created the world for a play,*
> *But found when He came to compose it*
> *That He really had nothing to say.*

Which was silly of course, for He was saying me still,
wasn't He? And Bessie. If my role this evening was to
take the bitch to the dog, then I was fulfilling God's will.
That Bessie (who is fond of the booze) had proved incapable of producing anything that ran faster than a three-
legged rabbit was just part of the mystery. Yet a great
bond existed between Bessie and myself and as we headed
for the village two moving dots on a lip of land shearing
away into endless waters, I would have been tempted to
see something heroic in us but for the echo of that celestial
chuckle that is ever-present now. A resident imp in a red
jacket and plumed hat tickles it out on my ear drum. If
gods there must be, my sceptical nature is better equipped
to deal with a band of rascals. That some hairy guy up
there in his cups concocted us in his image would make
quite good sense to me. The infinite goodness of the One
is the subject of at least two weekly trances.

Yet some instinct, perhaps of appeasement to a darker
vision that had loomed this evening, caused me to stop
with the village in sight and, passing my hand through
the warm air, scoop up a mile of the glittering tide.

'A present for you, Bessie,' I said. 'For your nuptials.'

But first a drink. Hogan's held no presentiment of dark
things. The pattern seemed quite usual for the time of
year. A bunch of young foreigners were loudly playing
rings. As I slipped with my pint into a corner beside
Andy O'Toole my sense of *deja vu* returned but sullenly,

full of its own peculiar torpor that probably had more to do with Andy's Buddha-like immutability than anything else.

Perhaps the young tourist girl had something to do with my staying on. If she hadn't looked the living image of my sister Eileen as a girl the evening might have taken a different turn. I would have escorted Bessie to her beau and afterwards sought out my own belle Joanie, as actually arranged, at the dance. But the leggy girl with eyes of cornflower blue affected me in a way that I had to have another pint, and from the sly looks Andy was giving her I was sure that he too had seen the resemblance. Andy had been in love with Eileen—or rather he had pined for her in such a state of frozen reverence that he came to be known in the family as Eileen's Standing Stone. He would remain motionless in a field for hours watching the cottage, a tall stout boy silent as the hill.

The stump of Andy's arm swung now as he reached for his drink. He had lost it in America and was steadily drinking his way through a small fortune in compensation. Beside me he bulked large and florid exuding a faintly rancid smell, a stunted man stealing glances at a mirage of his youth. We didn't have to say a word. It was what drew me to Andy—and appalled me too. Once we had shared a school bench and been called Mutt and Jeff. Here we were again every second night sharing a bench and we hadn't come very far. Years hence I saw the two of us sitting in the same corner over pints remembering not a girl but this evening when memory still held a sting.

Of course I hadn't quite written myself off yet. I had all my physical extremities, thank God. Such as they were, God help us. I had made trade, however much herself lamented my lack of Drive and Ambition which in any normal man would years ago have transformed two rural petrol pumps and a hole in the ground into a complex of automated machinery and gleaming showrooms. I had my haiku, which largely explained (I admit it) the nonexistence of the latter. And I had Joanie—or could have if I gave one or other of the extremities a bit of a push.

To give Joanie her due she was the first girl who ever kissed me willingly with her eyes open. Believe me, though I seem to have a fast comic line about my appearance, it has always been a real challenge with women, and I'm not running myself down merely to soothe my vanity. To be vain you must have something going for you and not be in a state of chronic standstill. That was it: I missed passion and I lacked adequate terms of sexual reference whereby I might know if I *should* have any. I felt desire, yes but it was strangely outside me, a cognitive thing, an awareness of potency but with no will to give gas. Perhaps I still harboured adolescent illusions about detecting some tell-tale touch of soul in the lip, subtle flavours of compatibility. But whatever it was the heart refused to flutter, and in this respect I was tempted to conclude that it was already banjaxed.

Yet on a higher level of sexual relativity I wondered how I could ever decide that I had gone off the women entirely when I had actually never been on them—apart from a few commercial transactions in Birmingham which involved no kissing, when I was learning my trade. For the sad fact was that I had spent most of my young manhood avoiding being stepped on by the taller ones. And where does passion go when the small ones see before them a bald maneen with buck teeth and a google eye and I swear to God it's a miracle I haven't a club foot?

Of course what really worried me was not so much the flowering of passion (which might come along nicely if I could refrain from conceptualising every fumble and grunt) but that for the mother and Bald Tyres (both peasants at heart) it was basically a question of *making a match* and damn the compatibility. If you're healthy hard-working people with respect for each other the liking will come. Better marriages were made on earth than ever fell from heaven. Thus runs that argument.

Frankly I thought it would be asking for trouble. For one thing I wasn't going to cease being a sceptic overnight (or when baby arrived) and what was going to happen when baby grew up and wanted me to hear his catechism? Was I going to split myself down the middle for the sake of Joanie who was born with a holy medal in her mouth? Imagine living in the same house with *two* saintly jobbers!

Then there was the question of my literary well-being. Was this to be jeopardised by forced-fed Drive and Ambition which as a family man wearing the bib and tucker of respectability I should muster to meet the approved norms of status and acquisition? For I know my Joanie. It was all nice and dandy talking to her about books and poetry but if you listened carefully to what she said, to her views on economies, domestic budgets, savings (a big item), you would know that while she's a very affectionate girl like a little round oven you could toast your toes to on a winter's night and maybe pop a bun in now and again, she has one hand delicately in God's muff while the other is neatly wrapped around her purse.

A good wife! one man might say. Another would simply turn away but—and this is the nub — Joanie was *the only woman in my life*. This made it a serious business. Dwell on the temptation, friend, to grab the only hot crumpet that's likely to come your way. With Bald Tyres maybe throwing in the cow. But was the real price (for what? a bedfellow? kids? putting me on the potty when I'm senile—maybe I'd be putting her on) a monstrous concession on my part to her bland conviction that a true man's mettle is forged in reason and not in the romance of words? How many fine spirits has the world seen throttled by the cold hand of common sense!

Like the other night after listening to me rattling on

after a few pints and maybe impatient too for there we were in a cosy ditch and I was doing nothing, she said, 'What a funny man you are, Michael.'

When you hear that you can mount your bicycle and forget about the other.

'Why funny?' said I.

'I mean, I can never think of you as a mechanic.'

In a nutshell! A quality of sadness, regret, lurked in her sweet voice, and what wouldn't that breed beside bairns? She meant I would never really believe in what I was doing. I would always be prouder of being a literary autodidact than a shrewd marketeer. Even when I tried to impress upon her that I actually liked cars I could see we were speaking a different language.

I *do* like cars. I like their refusals, the sound of their exasperation, their smells of human life, the tokens of people's existence in a glove compartment. Matter breathes, writhes. Read your Hopkins. Read Michael M. McNamara, haiku poet. Instress in every axle. Cars and the maintenance of the seventeen syllable eye.

'When I think of high octane, Joanie,' I said, 'I think of power, poetry! What we need are more high octane haiku. More women with a high antiknock rating.'

New cars, I told her, warming to my theme, were like brides confidently humming, strong. Older, they must be manipulated with much flattery which, like any veterans of the road, they at once see through. Really old, they must be bullied and loved in a different way.

'So cars, Joanie,' I concluded in my best Shavian manner, 'are female and cantankerous and must be treated accordingly. But that does not mean that I must sleep and eat with them.'

From the way Joanie was looking at the moon I could hear her wondering whether it might ever be a good idea to allow me to sleep with herself. There was no confident hum out of her anyway . . .

A ring rolled around my foot. I picked it up and handed it to a tall blond youth. Bessie had stretched out. She seemed totally indifferent to the prospect of union with Toby Jug, the local champion. A saucer of Guiness was more in her line and I got her one. She has a real weakness for the stuff. The young tourists pointed to her and laughed. It was so Irish. Was that how they saw Andy and myself, two silent locals with an alcoholic greyhound?

I eyed the clock. Soon I would have to take Bessie home and put on the dancing shoes. Joanie would be waiting with her friend Nora. They were replicas of myself and Andy, short and tall. We still met *at* places, at the hop, at the pictures. It wasn't quite going steady. Unsteady?

I had another pint and that threatened to disturb the immediate balance of things. Through a tumult of laughter over the rings the blue-eyed girl hugged the blond youth, kissed him. There was no doubt about the quality of their kisses. I ravished her with my eyes, the long brown thighs, the line of the young breast, her stance of careless abandon. Her freedom! Compared with Joanie, I thought cruelly, she was like a lovely lean chop. She looked at Bessie and then at me, and smiled.

A girl smiling through rings of laughter

I leant back in my corner and allowed words to drift.

Blue-eyed girl . . . Blue eyes of a girl.

A memory came to me swirling up through fronds and pebbles.

Blue eyes of a girl
Leaping through rings of laughter.
Eileen alanna.

Yes, in a stream. A small boy with two girls, their dresses tucked into their knickers. Turning up stones in a muddy mill race that joined the river, looking for eels which they speared with kitchen forks. Eileen's long face shivering in the pools, her pale legs stepping with heron grace among the weeds. I clung to them. There's one! Stick, stuck! The thing coiled and my heart twisted on the memory, hid from it among old tyres and wrecks, froze beside a patch of filthy oil on a puddle.

Had I been in a trance? The young people had left. So had Andy. I stood at the bar watching the dusky cream of a pint silting down into black. My beloved Eileen was dead, but it wasn't only that. Bitterness stabbed in me as if in that bowl of memory the present had crystallised with hateful clarity, its caricatures, its booming trivia. The carnival roared on the other side of the village. It was like a beast howling in the trees and I wanted none of it. The marquee would be filling up with dancers and I wanted none of that either. Who was I fooling? Did I really expect to be able to live with those two women?

I threw the birthday fiver on the bar and topped up Bessie's saucer.

Some time later on the road I let her off the lead and said, 'Go on! Plenty of rough trade around here. I don't care. Have a ball. Have a few.'

She was fuddled like myself but in a happier way. She licked my face. Never had she been out so late with me or been plied with so much booze. Maybe she thought it was her birthday. I had got Tom to soften the cap of a pint bottle and from this I poured a little into a hollow in the road. I must have had puddles on the brain. But Bessie was nowhere near me. The full moon lit up the fields. Passing the caravan site I saw a few lights, a man sitting on steps smoking his pipe.

'Hoor, Bessie!' I cried. 'The roaring gods are with us. Have it away where you can. Fornicate, my lovely!'

'In here, Michael,' said a voice from behind a wall, and a woman laughed.

I wandered on and then I was calling her. 'Bessie! Here girl!' A movement in a field caught my eye. It was Bessie racing around after something. I saw her roll over. She was fluthered. Climbing over the wall and breaking the bottle I ran towards her. Something small and white was running from her. A white rabbit? I stood and waited and eventually she came with the creature in her mouth shaking it vigorously from side to side. She swerved away from me when I tried to catch her. I heard tiny piping sounds and someone above on the road calling, 'Trixi! Trixi!' I threw myself on the dog and took from between her jaws a smooth-haired terrier pup.

I panicked. Blood flowed darkly over my fingers. The neck seemed to have been torn open. A few minutes later I realised my mistake—the blood was flowing from a cut on my own wrist—but then it was too late. I had knocked the pup's head against a stone, raced down to the cliff edge and flung it over. I collared Bessie and crouched in the tall grass. The voice continued to call, 'Trixi! Trixi!' but faded then back towards the caravan site.

What happened next was like something in a dream. I remember wrapping a handkerchief around my wrist and lying flat in the grass to light a cigarette. My heart was thudding. I had clouted Bessie a few times and she lay beside me whimpering. Then I was weeping myself, my head between my knees. Not since I was a little boy had I wept like this. The outside world was a distant ringing place. I had no sense of where I was and no immediate sense of a hand touching my shoulder. Then I looked up, recoiling. It was Hannah May, her cadaverous face close to mine, her hair wild against the moon. She was making a hissing sound and nodding her head.

'Clear off, Hannah May,' I said, rolling away from her. 'I've no drink, if that's what you're looking for.' But she remained, squatting on her hunkers and grinning at me. She was a miserable wretch who years before had lost her whole family in a fire and never got over it. She lived in a tumbledown cottage and some said she had become a

witch practising black rites. Others said she waylaid
drunken men on their way home and robbed them.

Again it was like a dream. For a long period I seemed
to ignore her, oblivious of everything but the stars and
the black line of the cliffs. Then she was there again like
an apparition and this time I cursed her, calling her a
witch and a whore and a cadger of drink and warning her
that if she didn't clear off I would have the priest on her.
I threw something, I remember, a stone or a bit of stick,
and she scuttled away.

Now Hannah May went over the cliff not twenty yards
from where we had been squatting. You might say that
it could have happened to her any night or that anyone
could have cursed her on her way, but when the mother
arrived in from Mass the next morning and said that her
body had been found on the rocks below Deasy's corner
I was shocked. Indeed nursing my sore head I had
completely forgotten about the encounter and for an
instant I went into a cold sweat at the thought that in my
drunken state I had flung her over. Then what I couldn't
get out of my mind was that with my vicious words
ringing in her ears the poor woman might have deliber-
ately thrown herself over. Perhaps she had just lacked
that final insult to make her do it. I thought of Andy, the
only one around who had any time for her. He gave her
money and drink and didn't care what people said. Could
I ever sit and drink with him again?

It was a bad Sunday all round. The mother and I
hardly spoke to each other. She couldn't get over my
high-handed decision not to take Bessie to the dog and
suspected, rightly, that I had gone into Hogan's and
remained there. I wandered far into the fields away up
past Jacko's Cross as if I wanted to put myself as far as
possible from the cliff edge. It was no use: I was pursued
by the picture of a poor wretch in tattered clothes falling
through the darkness to land like a rag doll among the

boulders. A remark from old Mrs. O'Connor, sunning herself beside her gate, further darkened my conscience.

'The poor crathur,' she said. 'Don't I remember ye all picking blackberries together on the road and sneaking into the garden there for an apple. A regular tomboy was Hannah May, God rest her.'

How one forgot! Other memories as if waiting on cue rushed upon me as I lay on a mossy bank: Hannah May siding with me in a fight, shielding me from a bigger boy; giving me a lick of her ice cream; standing with Eileen in a muddy stream, her dress tucked into her pink knickers, holding a kitchen fork. Was it to *her* legs I had clung?

I thought of a fine haiku by Ryota:

> *In the long hallways*
> *Voices of the people rise*
> *In the morning haze.*

What voices rose in the dusk now to torment me! If I were to die that day what would be my 'death verse'?

I am not dramatising. All that evening and the next day I carried around with me a sense of my own evil—or at least a sense of how far I had strayed from the radiance of my first hope when I had hurried home from Birmingham to work again among these fields. I couldn't get back fast enough away from plastic people, tellyache and the sour piss of Patrick's tribal sons—to what? To venting my maudlin anguish on a human wreck who may have wanted to comfort me (*she* comforting *me*!) as she had once done when I was a small boy? Yes, I was evil and no fancy words could cover it.

The sergeant called and there I lay under Hogan's old pick-up. I had made up my mind. A thought which a little earlier would have filled me with scorn, to wit, that a man really needs a woman to protect him from himself, now appeared eminently reasonable. It was a harbour we needed however buffeted by the squalls of temperament.

I was on my feet when Bald Tyres reappeared. He was

flushed from the whiskey she had been pouring into him
but he was also a little embarrassed.

'Joanie says she missed you at the dance,' he said.

'Aye, I didn't go.' He hesitated and it was on the tip of
my tongue to inform him there and then of my intentions
(I suddenly felt very formal about it) but he hurried off
at a shout from his driver on the road. Instead I wandered
in to tell herself. I sat at the table and waited for her to
come in from the back. Omar watched me with his love-
in eyes. It's all right, I told him. I'll be back in the fold
any day now. For peace sake, if nothing else.

Here she was in with a bucket. At the sight of her
self-satisfied expression my mood dipped again. She
looked like that when she'd got a red hot tip for the track.

'Well,' I said blandly to break the ice. 'What had Bald
Tyres to say for himself? He had a tip?'

She put down the bucket, wiped her hands on her
apron, gave me a long level stare and said, 'There'll be
no more Bald Tyres out of you now, sonny.'

'Why so?'

'Your attitude must change.'

'Must it?' I was stung by her calm anticipation. You'd
imagine I had already popped the question. 'How do you
know what my intentions are?'

'*Your* intentions,' she said, leaning towards me on the
table. 'What about *my* intentions?'

'Your intentions?' It was like ping-pong.

'Joe and myself,' she announced, 'are going to wed.'

I had stood up, now I had to sit down again. I felt as
if I had just swallowed a bingo ball. Tick-tock went the
clock. Bald Tyres the merry widower? And herself?
Courting under my nose? But of course! All those cups of
tea and racing for her teeth every time she spotted the
squad car. She was showing them now with her hands on
her hips and with an absurd pang of regret I fancied that
they were in for keeps surely.

I managed to find three words. 'Does Joanie know?'

'Nobody knows,' she said, looking terribly smug. 'That's the way it is now, boyeen,' she went on, pottering around again. So there'll be no more Bald Tyres out of you. The name is Joe'. She turned with the kettle in her hand. 'Why, do you think we're too old?'

I was aware of the photograph by the dresser but I kept my eyes on her and said, 'No, you're a fine woman still,' and then, looking at her erect figure, I realised that I meant it. What had grey hair to do with it anyway? 'And I'm to marry Joanie?' I added weakly, as if putting the question to myself.

'Faith then,' she said, laying the table, 'you may have been a little too slow on the turn there, child of grace. Joe says she met a nice young man on Saturday night. He drove her home, aroo, and they sat billing and cooing for hours in the car. Dick Tracey from the Pike. Do you know him?'

I did. Jesus, that fellow billing and cooing? A big yahoo with butter in his horn. She was welcome to him. A sense of great hilarity possessed me but I put on a doleful face. Then it was suddenly real for a terrible thought struck me.

'Tell me,' I said. 'Are you marrying out or is Ba . . . Joe marrying in?' No haiku that, Fred.

'What do you think?' she said. 'Of course I'm marrying out. Do you think we'd want a lazy article like yourself under our feet?' She jabbed a spoon at me. 'You've a free run at it now, gorsoon, and it's up to you to make something of it and not have me clucking around you all day like a mother hen.' Oh, misery! 'Show some drive and ambition and forget the pomes. Far from pomes we were reared. And it'll be up to you to find a woman for yourself. If I can find a man at my time of life surely you can find a woman or go shtone daft here on your own.'

'And if I never find her and go shtone daft?'

'Then we'll know for certain, sure.'

Alone! Wasn't it what I really wanted? To be my own sweet hillbilly? A vista of indolence (with just enough Drive and Ambition) opened to me. But how near I had come to losing it! What if I had opened my mouth to Joe alias B.T.?

I looked across at the Good Shepherd but I wasn't seeing him at all. Behind the fleecy clouds, sampling grapes on a soft Olympian rug, I saw a big bearded fellow rocking with laughter. Beside him stood a golden girl bearing a cup. It was Hannah May in all the glory of her youth. She raised the cup to me and smiled.

— Ha! But didn't I fool you! the fellow crowed, grape juice running over his chin.

— You bastard, I said. You cut things fine, you know. He was tickled pink.

— Do you realise what a close shave I had? I demanded.

— Aye, a great shtory altogether, he laughed. And what a nice little twischt I gave it there at the end. Didn't I now, child of grace?

Watching

You seem to have forgotten that I can't see very far, that these feathered creatures you are lined up watching are so often lost to me in the lake's shimmer, the blur of greens and browns. Yet I still raise my glasses and look as I used to when we first went bird-watching, when I wanted to share in whatever you were doing.

I was good at pretending. So carefully had I studied the pictures of the birds that when you said, 'See.' I saw and could tell what I saw, that pale stripe over the eye, the white underwing, the black throat, and truly the bird was there though frequently all I saw was a shape in a tangle of leaves. I had mastered my secret braille out of love. It was also a challenge. On cue I read movement, colours, *saw* perhaps more really as a blind man sees, the life on poles, fences, wheeling among the clouds. I found a line in one of the Upanishads that drifted through my happiness: That which needs no eye to see but sees, that alone is spirit, not what sets the world by the ears.

Where are we? Lough Owel? I glance at the map in the bus but within minutes of stopping I hardly know which lake it is—and we have been here so many times. It is a place. And I come for other reasons now, to walk, to breathe this air. I am rather tired of my braille, and now you never say, 'See?'

I watch the people. Some I greet from past outings and chat while we straggle over to a vantage point, helping each other over gates, holding down barbed wire. But there is a reserve that checks familiarity. The words we speak do not encroach as if it were natural for us to share with the birds a heightened sense of our own territories. The ones that annoy are clever in their knowledge. You hear it in their voices. 'What masses of shoveler!' that woman exclaims in her superior way.

Or is it envy? I am never the first to say anything.

Now we're at Owel. You stand rapt. What is it? A party of goldeneye? Telescopes are set up on tripods and the younger members of the group line up to look. It was what surprised me when I first went out watching with you, how many young people are interested. I was under the impression that all bird-watchers were eccentric old gentlemen in plus fours.

I raise my glasses and the choppy waters spring at me, peak, spurt. No, I think of Hopkins, they are *plucked* from the grey bowl of the lake. And somewhere I see them, the brave family of goldeneye bobbing along, especially the duck with her white collar. Beside me a young couple, beginners, shyly consult their book. They remind me of us then, though of course we never brought a book along, you were far too knowledgeable. I did all my homework afterwards.

That one, I want to say, yes, that's the goldeneye. The young man glances at me. Back off, lady. We'll find it.

I step back from the line. All silent now, intent, as if expecting some great event. I move forward again and stand just behind your right shoulder. Your bulk. Most of it is the new sheepskin. You have a black man's grey head. If I didn't know you now with your collar up I would say you were a black.

'Yes,' a young voice says. 'I see them. Oh, lovely.' And foolishly I want to reach out and touch you and say goodbye, just like that, and thank-you, for maybe later I will never feel like saying it just like that again standing, apart, all my senses alert and the March wind whipping away the sadness of it and the pathos. Even if you didn't hear it or understand I would have said it and when I'm lying in the hospital I would remember. I dread saying it then, the voice slurring over thought, seeing you through a haze. But maybe the operation is no more serious than the doctor says. Do you know? Is it all a conspiracy to make me believe? Don't be daft, you say. Why should we hide it from you? (My infamous 'nerves'?) You that never wanted to delude or be deluded?

'A grebe.'

Ah, didn't I!

'Where?'

'Just in line with that tree over there, the one that's . . .'

'I see it.'

A Great Crested Grebe, is it? Somewhere I see it but as a boat, a Viking, the proud sail thrusting swan-like past the shore. Perhaps I loved the names first and then the words: rufous-bellied, golden-fronted, fulvous-naped, the soft plumage of champions. And that was how you used to talk of them. You used to *talk*. They possessed the earth. Or what was it you liked to say? They were the real conquistadores but enriching what they found by their very presence, the true guests of the nation, and we pay them the greatest compliment of not interfering with them, defending their habitats with no motive other than to see them there, to watch over them.

'Tufted duck.'

'Yes, quite a few.'

What lofty sentiments then! How you hated the mere 'ticksters' adding rarities to their life-list, and the mean watchers who begrudged the club a few quid a year but wanted it all done for them. But you are selfish now too, aren't you? The birds are an alibi for silence, or for the fewest possible words, simple ones that tell what you see, therapeutic words, naming, directing, policemen's words stripped of all that is not functional.

Words, birds. How close they sound. You escape from one to the other, for you are sick of words, outside them. You come home hollow-eyed from smoky rooms full of union talk and haggling where words are vanes of windmills and younger men are tilting at you. You are afraid of being discarded by the world. Can I blame you for your silences? Now you use words as spanners, keys. Or you dispense them with that politeness behind which you hide. You have become correct in words. They serve you in your meticulous love for your wife and family. Is it one of the things we discover: how our use of words makes or destroys us? How we grow to suspect them and cease to want to communicate what springs from the heart, or love them and still try?

It is much more, isn't it? The young couple beside us think it is all fusion and togetherness. They will blame their rows on misunderstandings. You don't love me anymore, she will cry. What she will discover is that the absence of love is usually only the inability to convey a certain *kind* of love, as one species of bird is incapable of emulating another. Doesn't it seem unfair that there aren't recognisably different species of people?

I turn back down the path towards the railway line angry with myself. Even if this were our last outing (and I'm not worrying, even as I write this) I had resolved not to be elegiac. I was going to walk, pick up a stone or two. But isn't that just as dishonest? Wasn't it melodramatic to want to touch you just now and say good-bye. Would we cringe if we saw it in a film? Yet I wanted to do it.

The light spikes the trees, holds aloft the image of our lives wrung from us at last. There it is caught up in the branches, an old rag. It kept us warm, fed us. I can see that. It kept us tender in our silence doing things for each other. How bad it was! Yet on the way up to the lake all

I could think was how more naturally I can touch you when we walk.

The line is breaking up. Time for sandwiches and tea laced with rum. My pain. My pills.

Before me the young couple. I cannot seem to avoid them. I go down a different path yet there I am again on their heels! 'No pochard,' I say, idiotically, turning aside. They glance back at me fearing my determination to be their guide. How cold they look, and discouraged. So far they have hardly seen a bird they could name without consulting their little book. They hug each other and kiss, a long jerky walking kiss that ends in a splutter of laughter.

I stop and train my glasses on nothing, on the sky, a cloud resembling a plume of smoke from a factory. I think of Blackpool. Remember? You were at conference and I was one of the wives. We visited a factory. Down the production line we trailed, you bending over to catch the facts shouted in your ear. I picked up a pair of ear phones and the noise fell away. I was in a cave in which something hissed with a regularity I found hypnotic. The young machine operator nodded at me and smiled. I thought of words as human things waiting in the locker rooms, waiting to jump at him and embrace him. 'Yes,' you said later in the hotel room, 'but every job has its price.'

That was the period when I came closest to hating you. You were suave. I watched you from the balcony of the Winter Gardens, listened to you speak. You looked like an exotic bird with your greying hair and rich dark beard. Seated among the wives I waited for you to look up and smile, and your smile when it came was for them as much as for me. You looked full and sleek and your words were silky. You were sucking in power and it flowed to you, crackled about you like electricity. Women wanted to touch you, to dance. And all I could think of was that you had found your price. I moped around Blackpool.

Someone on the deserted beach had traced I WAS HERE. I remember wondering what blind faith had guided the hand. Who was I? And then I allowed that young American to tumble me. After coffee we wandered into his room as if it was the most natural thing in the world. He couldn't have been much older than our Jim at the time. Why? The sex? That was a laugh. I felt incestuous. To get back at you? To move afterwards graciously and with my own power among the wives in their print dresses? Later I saw that I had wanted to abase myself. I was the observer on the balcony with clean hands, smelling of roses. I was priceless.

Have I contrived all these words merely to confess my pecadilloes? That would be a joke, wouldn't it? They are such distant things, specks in the sky that could be anything.

You approach, your head tilting in that worried way when you see me standing looking at nothing, smiling to myself.

'Hungry?' you say.

'A little.'

'What's so amusing?' Am I still smiling?

'That young couple,' I say, linking you. 'They think I'm a mother hen out to take them under my wing.'

Food. A rustling of paper all down the bus. In this we are at one with the birds, with all of nature. What have they travelled hundreds of miles for if not a bit of grub, a little warmth. This is the way the world should be, how you would have it: no great flights of fancy, not much of that concern with art and poetry that has marked me down in the family as a hopeless romantic, but a place of reason and discipline in which each has his own territory, his sandwiches and flask. Willing to share of course as a good human. Only here no one shares. The young wife is just across the aisle. I am tempted to offer her some of our whiskey salami but I don't dare. I would make matters worse, probably cling to them after all in my efforts to convey that I wanted to do nothing of the kind. I am like that. With you as well. I would not fill our silence, I would overflow it if you gave me half a chance, become excited, perhaps weep, the unpardonable sign of my 'nerves'. So you stick to your tender, meticulous, policemen's words. Your gentle, hollow words.

'Good cheddar this.'

'Yes, whatever it is. It was in a plain wrapper.'

Hand me this, hold that, wipe the other. This is the way words should be used. It is the way we die.

'Any tissues?'

'Four.'

Not a couple, or a few. Four. You are like that.

You chew in my ear, looking around. I used to hate it. And the way you suck in your breath when you eat and talk. The young man slips down in his seat, pretends to be a chick being fed by his wife. The man who looks a bit like you in another sheepskin coat whispers something in his companion's ear. He smiles. You sit stiff, observant. I must prepare you to touch you. Watch out, here I come with my hand.

'What is it?'

'Cheesy crumb. Don't want to get it into the leather.'

A branch claws at the window. In a cottage garden a woman bends down. The young ones chatter at the rear.

'Good the taste of the rum tea with the whiskey salami.'

'Hmm.'

'Must get more.'

'Hmm-hmm.'

I think of magpies. After Blackpool they seemed to congregate in our garden to mock me. Sly, scheming things. That was the worst time. The drinking, the shrieks. I overflowed then. The children shooting up, out, always out. I became allergic to sounds. The priest's voice was a dirge. God was a kookaburra laughing at us all day, wondering how close we will come to him, whether we'll catch even a glimpse of his tail before he flits away. The radio was animate, a head alive with jingly things that made me feel dirty inside. The Arabs were punching holes into all your fine speeches. Every day your words were being hurled back at you.

Yet it was then, when you were losing faith in words, that I discovered in them a kind of salvation. It was the mistake you all made thinking it was the peace of the nursing home that had brought me back to myself. One day I sat on a bench beside a man who was reading the poems of Mallarmé. I had never seen him around the grounds, and after our encounter I never saw him again. Indeed later I fancied he was an angel sent down to change me with a few words. Not a magic formula. When I talked of myself, of the me that drank and smoked and stared and ranted he thought for a while and said, 'Yes, but can't you see this "me"? Can't you see it standing there demanding all these explanations and roles and fulfilment?' 'Yes,' I said. 'Of course I can.' 'So you can observe yourself?' 'Yes, I can.' He stood up and I thought he was going to leave it at that. But he turned and said, 'How can you be that which you observe?' And he walked away with his book under his arm.

What a success I was when I came home. It was the rest, you all said. I had got out of myself. You all looked so happy I dared not say that I was only discovering how to get *in*. You made love as if it was your duty, as if I expected it. And I did, and wanted it. But you were changing too. Your lips and eyes had hardened, and your heart. My new-found enthusiasm for poetry was part of my 'nerves'. Ever afterwards I was marked by that visit to the home. When we made love I saw parallel lines that touched giving off sparks that flew like fiery swifts but then ran smooth and cold again. In this 'I' behind the rapacious 'me' the man revealed I had found a still, immutable part in me that watched everything, watched the watchers, but it was so fleeting, so similar to the birds that were *almost* there, just out of focus, that to speak of it would have been to sound neurotic again, perhaps even schizophrenic. Yet I could have tried more, couldn't I? I acquiesced too easily, drifting into my 'aesthetic' world, abandoning all you sturdy extroverts to the 'real' one.

'Where to now?'

'Glen Lough, I think.'

Glen Lough. I would not mistake this place, perhaps because I see it as a real sanctuary, a place the birds come when the bigger lakes are too rough. No waves here, no majesty of line, rather a furlough in the dip of soft fields. Homely too with the presence of the heavy white-fronted geese. Even I can see them.

On the boreen leading to the lake a tinker lad, his hair streaming, scatters the group on his old piebald. His vitality is a rebuke to us in our capes and leggings. In a cottage doorway a woman, her arms folded, looks amused. What idiots from the city are we out on a day like this?

'Only two mallards here today seemingly.'

'Oh, shellduck!'

'Yes, we're lucky.'

I stand and look at the light, look and look, letting it suck out my darkness till I am nothing but a shell. We are dying in the whip and snap of March. More words. Once, grandiloquently, I wrote in my diary, 'Words when loved recall us to reality, raise our lost white selves from the lake bed, and miraculously we walk again.' I look out upon the lake and feel nothing but the silence behind the wind. How good it is!

'Four pintail moving left.'

'Yes, I see them. Pursued by lapwing.'

'Rather scarce here, pintail.'

The therapeutic words emptying self, riveting the eye

on what is simply there, what moves and feeds. Light showers upon the water. Shoveler.

'What masses of shoveler!' the woman cries.

'Geese coming down by the whooper.'

'Lovely.'

A tinker child watches us from a tree. The geese are up again. What startled them? Are there fish among those reeds? I look up again and the realities are stilled, immense in their simplicity: water, fish, birds, grass, us and the child in the tree like a different species of us wondering how close she can come, if we would accept her presence. You. Me. And this changeless 'I' watching it all.

At Derravarragh, our last stop, the light fading, I glimpse what it is. We are behind time. It is after six and the bus was to have been back in the city by half-past. Yet even now a move is on to see the pochard someone has sighted farther down the shore. The young couple glance at each other in dismay. They are cold, hungry. What addicts are these? Haven't we seen enough? The wife looks at me as if I were to blame. Have I been going around like a silly old bag urging everyone to find the pochard?

You have wandered over a small stream that feeds the lake. I watch you climbing a hillock. I wander. *I wander by the edge/of this desolate lake*. The Children of Lir haunted these waters. I raise my glasses that are misted over and blind, and see them crossing the face of the moon. And I close my eyes, and for an instant fatigue, pain are forgotten. I feel a warmth, a wholeness in the drift of space and time. The stars wheel. We are shapes, and in that deathless part of us, perfect. I open my eyes and look across to you.

I *see* you!

A hand touches me. You are beside me, head tilting.

I have been watching the other man who looks like you. And they come, after all, the tears. The unpardonable.

Homeward bound. The young couple appear to have quarrelled. They sit erect, silent. But we have merged. Does it matter that you are asleep, your stiff old head sunk deep into me?

Friends and Occasional Lovers

It was his voice she heard, days after their walk, as if it were a prism she could hold against even the most familiar scene and see it transformed. She recalled his words as they stood and watched the boys diving above the lock. He saw them, she had felt at the time, as would a painter drawing from the white limbs, the movement, some hidden force that moved him. Or his description of the abattoir he had visited for his firm, the men through a mist of blood suddenly breaking into a wild 'Yahoo!' that travelled down the line, a human cry rising above the relentless slaughter. In bed she heard it below her window echoed in a drunken yell that was taken up farther down the street and yet again out towards the bay where they had stood gulping air after a dance, close to the piping of the oyster catchers. And for a moment men slick with blood still prowled the city venting their spirit and contempt.

Yet on that first morning when Betty awoke he was confused with other people she had met at the party and their arrangement to meet for a walk was unreal, part of a tipsy scheme. A German called Otto, a 'roving watchdog' for his firm, he could rove, she thought, turning over. He was one of several faces already receding as on the stern of a holiday cruiser. A spy most likely, she fancied, and wove a story around him as she drifted back to sleep.

But on Sunday mornings her mother's sighs held a

note of sibilant prayer, a reminder that she had not yet given up the battle for her daughter's soul. The walk offered an immediate goal. He was interesting in his rather intense way, and for a married man on the loose quite correct. Of course she had been aware that this could be his smooth continental way of talking her into bed. She had challenged him when he dropped her off at her door and suggested a walk: 'Why do you want to see me again?'

'As a friend,' he said, smiling and offering his hand as though to seal a bargain. She thought she might just keep him to it.

From Baggot Street bridge she saw him standing by the lock where boys sported in the water. Swept by a burst of sunlight her mood turned carefree. She felt in command and held out her hand in formal greeting.

'Is that where you run the tourist business single handed?' he said, pointing to a building on the far side of the bridge.

'That's right.'

'Do you swim in the canal too?'

'You must be joking.'

They sat on the grass and smoked. Beside him she felt small and frail and when he spoke she made a point of looking him squarely in the eyes which she saw were brown, flecked with yellow. But her eyes were drawn to the grey streak in his beard and his out-jutting lower lip the colour of ruby wine.

'Like small white frogs,' he said, observing the boys. 'In, out, jup, jup. Look at them. Something that's locked up in dark streets has been released into the sun and air. Very strange, watching them I could tell that they're not middle-class boys. It's not the same kind of energy.' She wondered if she would have made any such distinction. He looked at her and added, 'You're smiling because you think here's another German that wants to get to the bottom of everything he sees.'

'Let's walk,' she said, taking command again. 'Is it a myth then that Germans want to solve a problem when they see one?'

'No, I suppose that's in us,' he agreed. 'It's what intrigues me about this country. Two and two can make five and people laugh at it.'

'Do they?'

'I mean, there's a kind of . . . what should I say? . . . natural cycle to problems, a self-sorting-out.'

'You surely don't admire that.'

'Oh but I do!'

'In your companies as well?'

'Of course not. But life is bigger than companies and productivity. In this city I experience a natural rhythm of communication which, believe me, is precious. I always feel something will happen to me, someone will come up to me while I stand at a corner.'

'A beggar, most likely.'

He glanced sharply at her and said, 'You're so aggressive.'

'Am I?' she said with a shrug. They passed an artist who had set up her easel beside the path. 'Just like Paris, isn't it?' Betty laughed. Crossing over at Leeson Street bridge he held her bare arm and she tensed but relaxed again at once. When they were half way across he released her and they continued along the canal path. He talked of other impressions the city had made on him. Sipping shandies in a lounge bar beside the next bridge, he said, 'Even this, what do you say, plush? Carpets and plush seats in a bar.'

'And butts, matches and papers littering the floor.'

'Yes! Two and two make five!'

He analysed the impression a barman had made on him when, past closing time and yelling at people to the point of insult to go home, he yet carried on pulling pints and chatting amiably to someone. 'As if the man had two faces, like Janus,' or as if his cries had entered his blood like those of a street vendor. Betty relaxed in that sense of gracious yielding to a stranger's interest in the ways, the quaint anarchy, of her country. Why harp on the ignorance, the malignities? All aggression towards the man and her rôle as companion had faded. Indeed, looking around the sun-filled bar she marvelled how sane and mature it was to talk with people, to stroll with a complete stranger and share the life around. For a moment she even fancied herself commended by her Tourist Board bosses for exemplifying the very hospitable presence to which the nation so self-righteously aspired.

So it jarred strangely to be told that Otto's father was buried in Ireland, in the German war cemetery at Glencree. It was as if he had revealed a claim to the earth on which she stood, was himself through his dead father part of it. She felt rebuked for her condescension, and even coloured, though Otto did not appear to notice as he recalled his first pilgrimage to the country, as an orphan of sixteen, to find his father's grave.

'I thought I was the only German in the whole place,' he said. 'When I walked into a restaurant and found a bus load of them I was disgusted.'

She smiled and said, 'Poor Otto,' but he had opened a wound and in the days that followed—even in the bus to which she had run, leaving him abruptly with a wave back at the bridge—she probed it, brooding less on her own fugitive father buried somewhere in Coventry than on the confusion of her feelings about him. What pilgrimage had she undertaken? At most a desultory search for old photos her mother may not have destroyed. A drunken, deserting father, yes, but then how often had she in turn wanted to desert her mother, to run from those sighs, those looks of gentle reproach that after all the sacrifice

to put her through college she should have turned out
such a pagan, so 'unhappy' in herself! To what estate of
guilt and anger was she succeeding as to her true
patrimony?

From her office she could see the lock. No boys dived
and shouted but she saw them in the shadows white and
fleeting, as she saw Otto spying from some niche in every
plush lounge she entered. She banished him, thought of
his wife and children, his age, the other girls he undoubtedly picked up on his travels, but all remained faceless,
characterless, and at night he returned, his voice saying
nothing very clever but worming something different from
the familiar, and she wondered what he was watching
over and how. He mutated, becoming a real watchdog
with a silver chain called Otto, and one morning when
she awoke she saw him, fresh-faced and nervous, descen-
ing the gangway from the boat, a tall dark German youth
fumbling with the mysterious Irish tanners and bobs and
half-crowns.

On the day Betty received her full licence she bought
a second-hand car. The next evening after work she drove
out to the cemetery at Glencree. A mountain stream
bounded through a fir grove and belied the stillness, the
sense of being in a tiny amphitheatre hollowed from the
rocks. The graves shared a neat bed of heather marked
only by low pairs of crosses and the stone plaques along
the paths. To the left on entering was a shallow cave in
which uneven lines of golden inlay described Mary holding Jesus. An inscription in German meant nothing to
her.

But war sent me to sleep in Glencree.

The line from a poem inscribed on a plain standing
stone followed her among the paths. She pondered the
word 'war' and felt that it conveyed nothing, or rather
something reduced to the mechanics of melodrama.
Documentaries were as unreal as the bombs signalling

their havoc from far below. Standing, she closed her eyes
and wondered what the end might have been for some of
the men buried beneath her feet. She saw a plane ditching,
heard in the rush of air the keen of death approaching,
glimpsed a shape drifting into the silvered waves. But
again she had borrowed the scenario, it was the sound of
the stream coursing through her blood, and opening her
eyes she saw a sunken glade closer to the enchantments
of Irish myth, to the spirits of sacred well and thorny
bush and a faith as fine and luminous as the Woman in
the cave holding her golden Son as would an ancient
goddess of the underworld.

She studied the plaques and tried to recall his, the
father's name. It eluded her and for some reason this
moved her more than anything. In the end, as if in
atonement, she placed a few wild flowers beside a plaque
marked *Ein deutscher Soldat*.

But whatever she had expected from this little pilgrimage—and on the way home she chided herself for her
sentiment: what had she felt, even while laying the flowers, beyond a sense of wonder that she was there at
all?—the ghosts of the fathers, far from taking solace in
her interest, appeared to resent it. They taunted her.
'You couldn't even remember my name!' cried the German ghost shooting past in a small black cloud. And her
father's ghost, hidden in a tree, said sadly, 'What flowers
for me in my concrete tomb?' Once, looking out upon the
canal, she saw two old duffers coming down the path.
They appeared to be very drunk and had their arms
around each other. But when she looked again a moment
later they were gone. She waited. Were they behind a
tree? They never reappeared.

'You're looking pale,' Mrs. O'Dowd said to her. 'Aren't
you eating?'

Inside she felt pale. She thought her life was very
complicated. She had broken off with Joe Moran, the

apple of her mother's eye. He had all sorts of virtues, indeed he had been It until one day, as in a flash of second sight, she saw him turning into an incorrigible fusser. Their parting was more elevated. She had argued that they were too alike and thus cancelled each other out 'like noughts and crosses.' Far from wanting to merge with a man, she wanted him to be a dynamo to set off her own 'distinctness'. Joe, woeful dynamo, was struck dumb. From a distance Betty fumed at him. Why hadn't he demanded that she set *him* off? Why indeed hadn't he felt insulted? That he was suffering from piles hadn't helped.

On a cool windy day, eating her sandwich by the sea front, she perceived that for the first time consciously her adult past was beginning to mock her. It *was* a past now. Her student days were receding like the tail light of a train she had once travelled in. She called herself to book on the attitudes she liked to flaunt—such as her lecture to Joe, what had she *meant* by 'distinctness'? Was it just a word—the emancipated stance so readily adopted but rather as an obligatory mental exercise over a heart that lurched towards indifference? Beneath the swift play of images she was growing inert. To an old student friend she wrote, 'My head rattles with the grit of mere attitudes.' Her friend, newly-married and happy and born again to faith, offered predictable advice.

About three weeks after their walk a box of roses was delivered to the office, causing a flurry of interest. This was class. And who was this Otto who wrote (and whose card they all contrived to read): I thought of you today and of our walk by the canal. She shrugged him off as a crazy man—stunning Heather Lambe looked at her as if to say, 'Who'd give an ordinary thing like you roses?'—but it came as a relief and was, she knew, the prelude to another visit. This time, inevitably, it would be different.

The notion of an affair came to her as literary and

contrived, then more realistically as a scale of options with degrees of furtive passion and soul-searching at one end and a certain enlightened, carefree giving at the other. She saw them being enlightened about it, visiting places together, perhaps meeting in Amsterdam and walking by other canals or in Paris sharing a heap of mussels washed down by cool white wine. To share and possess but not to hold. Behind recessions, horrors, didn't people still do that? The affair would have that edge of scorn for the conventional pitfalls that were so obvious. She hit on a formula that sounded like the title of a sophisticated story. They would be, she thought, Friends and Occasional lovers.

When Otto did call and they arranged to meet in a small Greek restaurant he arrived looking jaded and smelling vaguely of wet sheepskin and disinfectant. He had flown in to demonstrate and supervise a new method of taking sheep's blood aseptically for his firm's diagnostic products.

'Can you smell me?' he said. 'Your nostrils are working.'

She had been thinking of another title, In the Shadow of the Slaughterhouse.

'Very slightly.'

'I did change but these clothes are full of it too and my shoes . . .'

'Never mind,' she said. 'It's much better than aftershave.'

He described his work but in such factual detail that she was soon lost. She felt deflated. From waiting for him tense and girlish (probing the sexual tension she had built up about the man) she became again detached and a little ashamed. It was as if she had got her dates mixed and the lover she had been expecting turned out to be a weary and preoccupied uncle in a smelly jacket. And his manner was faintly avuncular. Was he boring her? Had he embarrassed her by sending flowers? 'Young kids' didn't do that any more, did they? Under the wall lamp he appeared drawn. The wrinkles around his eyes were more deeply etched and the white scar in his beard looked tender and livid.

Strolling around the Green he was more like the self she remembered, commenting on things, faintly mocking, talking easily about his family, his wife who designed costumes for the theatre. He was solicitous, offering his arm as though to promenade on this elegant pavement were still a social mode. A certain formality seemed important to him and she worried about its genuineness. Was he conveying that he had every intention of keeping his original promise just to be friends? A companion in a strange city to fill the lonely hours? But by their touch, however formal, they were even now intimate. Passers-by would take them for lovers or man and wife. Intellectual affairs, she reflected, stopping to look through the railings, only happen in books or in heaven. Yet if such *were* indeed his wish, then she would be required a) to respect it or b) to frown upon it as rather suggesting that she posed no sexual temptation whatever. If a) wasn't he being a shade naive and literal? If b) he could take a running jump into a vat of sheep's blood!

I thought of you today. Not an overture to the heart?

In the crush of a pub on Merrion Row he stemmed his broad back against encroachments on her space in the corner, delicately picked a hair from her shoulder, explained the German electoral system. Even at the height of the melee the gap between their bodies remained inviolate, chaste. Sitting on the loo, Betty worked out c) which was that he might consider her virginal and Catholic and thus with no honest option *but* companionship to which she should be mature enough to respond. (If such were the case it should indeed be ennobling and refreshing after her experience of the married men who had slobbered over her their eloquent lust—but that was not what she wanted *now*). And d) which suggested that he was a smooth-talking German cook whose style was to keep girls in all kinds of places on the intellectual boil until they flowed over into his lap. However, this could just mean that while he did in fact want her he was keen to her awareness of his promise, allowing her the prerogative of breaking it.

But how? 'Just lean across and kiss him, silly girl!' said her father while she washed her hands. 'He's just being rather stiff and Germanic. Some of 'em are so straight you want to knock them crooked.' Yes, and then his ardour will suddenly, magically, erupt? Where the hell was it now? And anyway why should she be the first, like some punk rocker, to show passion? Where was the comehither in this quiet man's eyes, his cool quizzical nordic blood? If he were Latin (even Irish, God help us) wouldn't he be setting about actively beating down her defences? Or should the emancipated girl not have any, stand there like a grinning nudie on a shelf waiting to be handled?

'Can you drive?' he said, anxiously, when they returned to her car.

'Expertly,' she said, though she was feeling the effect of the gins on top of the wine. She had plumped for the German cook (the notion of a paternal being, a kind of wise diagnostic Faust, hovered somewhere but she ignored it) and felt antagonistic. All the way back to the hotel she hardly said a word. When she pulled into the car park they sat for a while and smoked. Now, churlishly, she waited in silence. At last he said, 'You're wondering about us, aren't you?'

'No, I'm counting my money.'

'The flowers and everything. What we are, or could be, to each other. If you don't want to see me again, Betty, I'll understand.'

'Do you want to see *me* again, Otto?'

'Of course.'

'Why?'

'Because . . . I . . .'

'Say it, for God's sake!'

'Because I desire you.'

'Bravo! Why is it so difficult for you to say so? I didn't *insist* on mere friendship, did I? The very fact that I agreed to see you again . . .'

'I was afraid of you.'

'What?!'

'You change so quickly,' he said. 'All the time we've been together it's like that. You go from being warm and comradely to aggression as if you wanted to eat my face away.'

'That bad?'

'Terrible.'

'Oh dear.'

'You don't see yourself. Perhaps you think you're shining with joy when you're pointing at me like a dagger.'

'Why didn't you say anything?'

'How? I thought you might walk away.'

'I just wanted to know what you really think.'

'You fascinate me,' he said. 'You're like the Irish weather.'

'Thank you *very* much.' She threw her head back and laughed. 'And you're like the Rhine, deep and smooth and smelly and I wonder if you have any passion at all, at all.'

'My passion is there,' he said, earnestly.

'Where?' She glanced back as if he had left it on the back seat. 'I'm sorry, I didn't mean to mock.'

'I mean . . .'

'Take me, Otto,' she said, staring up at the roof of the car.

He paused for a moment and said, 'No.'

'Why not? You think I'm drunk? I mean it!'

'Perhaps you do but we're both too outside of passion now . . . I mean, we're too mad about passion, to distrusting it, to mad *at* it . . . . to make it.'

'Make it?'

'Love, I mean.'

'You sweep me offa my feet, darling!' She turned to him, angrily. 'It's what you *wanted* to do, isn't it?'

'Yes, of course.'

'Well, then?'

'Like this . . . I mean, you do too?'

'I too do.' She pursed her lips. 'Kiss me, darling Otto.'

'Wait,' he said. Both were beginning to shake with laughter. 'The passion.'

'Where have you left it now?'

Holding on to each other they entered the foyer of the hotel. Betty marched straight across to a floor manager in a smart suit and said, 'We'd like a bowl of mussels and a bottle of dry white wine sent up to our room, please.'

'Certainly, madam,' the man said. 'Room number?'

Betty, fazed, looked around for Otto.

'Two hundred and seven,' he said, taking her by the arm and leading her towards the lift. Their mirth had suddenly drained from them and they stood like strangers beside each other waiting for the doors to open. A few other people entered with them and all remained silent on the way up. Otto watched Betty from the corner of his eye. She stood very pale and rigid, staring at the light flicking up from floor to floor. When the door opened she said, 'Otto . . .'

'I know,' he said. 'Come, quick. This door.'

She rushed into the bathroom and was immediately sick.

'That's it,' he said, holding back her hair. 'Good.'

'I'm sorry, Otto.'

'Don't try to talk,' he cautioned. 'I saw you going pale.'

He flushed the toilet and wiped her with a towel. 'You're over-excited.'

'Am I?' she said like a small girl. She was trembling and he wrapped her in the bed cover sitting up against the headboard and cradling her. The waiter came with the wine and mussels. It was like a bad joke. Otto ordered coffee. Through spasms of shakes Betty described a day she spent on the cliffs of Moher. In October. It was so cold and the wind from the sea so strong that it blew a stream tumbling down over the cliff edge back up into the air like a geyser. And up beside the tower they were able to lie back upon the wind as if they were elevating.

Otto told of being alone in a tent during a storm in the Black Forest. He had a magnum of wine and as the storm howled he drank from it but with no sense of becoming drunk since the elements raging around seemed infinitely the stronger force. When he finally emerged from the tent he fell flat on his face in the mud.

She hugged closer to him, feeling his warmth seep into her. The coffee arrived and they sipped it scalding hot. His beard was like a warm purring cat against her cheek.

'Tell me a little about everything, Otto,' she said.

'Won't your mother be worried?'

'No, she goes to bed very early.'

He talked a bit about his earliest memories, gathering coals along the railway line with his mother whom he barely remembered. Once a big GI gave him a bar of chocolate and he thought the man was more than human, a creature from another planet. He told of going to Mass with his first wife, a Catholic, in a small village church. When Mass was over the Protestant service began. And at night they slept over stables where the horses' chains rattled and getting into the feather bed was like slipping beneath the breast of a great white bird.

The steam from the mussels on the side table curled and died. Betty had a sensation of great space opening around her, a wide plain on which they and the scenes they evoked flowed in upon each other and became one. In the rising heat of their flesh they kissed and found each other, throwing aside the covers. But he came quickly and she closed her eyes, feeling cheated. Opening them again she saw him sitting back on his hunkers looking shamefaced, the sac of his passion dangling like a silly cock's wattle. Stretching out her arms she drew him down and said, 'Now we can be friends.'

When she awoke he was asleep in the twin bed. Noiselessly she dressed, sprinkled her face and crept from the room. The hotel was coming alive. A few American tourists were studying maps in a corner of the foyer. Betty stood beside her car and breathed in the air. An autumnal sky girded itself in ice-blue light. Leaves danced around her feet. She looked along the windows of the fifth floor. Soon the room would be vacant. She saw their spirits lingering, cherishing words. It occurred to her that she still did not know Otto's second name.

But we are benign spirits, she said to herself as if settling something. And as she whirled away down the tree-lined streets the thought was like a blessing on the city, on all the people and ghosts that dwelt there.

Sweet William

Damn the woman, Willy Featherstone fumed, striding along the pier. Damn all women and their damn functions. Of course men had it easy. True, men were not women. But would the fool see another doctor at least? No, she clung loyally to old watery-eyed Dr. Foley just because they played bridge together and he had seen them safely through all their little illnesses. But if you looked behind his ears you'd see the cobwebs, and as for hormones the man wouldn't recognise one from a horsefly. Foley's mother had apparently gone through the change as if she was stepping through a hoop, and so had *her* mother, Miriam insisted, so why shouldn't *she?* 'No reason at all,' Willy said to the gulls, 'except she's no one's mother but her own.' Which didn't make much sense but what did anymore? Miriam of course didn't want to believe that she had it at all, she was too young! It was all vanity, family pride and bull.

They were a devoted couple. The regulars on the pier were quite used to seeing them strolling along hand in hand. Now it seemed to be outside their control. As Miriam got worse Willy had a vision of hormonal armies waging constant war. It was as if Miriam's nature baulked at this natural transition, stood blushing and fretful at the portal of age refusing to enter (as indeed he imagined the horsy women of his own family having done) at a smart clip. Her mood went from melancholia to shrieks and back again. 'We're all knackered,' he said to a sad old duffer leaning against the pier wall. The man nodded in complete agreement.

Still, Willy blamed himself for having made the situation worse. Left to herself Miriam might well have coped, opening blouse and window when the flush was hot, closing same when cold, chucking the odd saucepan around, cuffing the Professor (their son), scolding Hanni the au pair, and eventually finding her old form. But he had to hurry things along. Perhaps the fact that neither of them, tall robust people, had ever been really ill lent an edge to his impatience. He wanted it over and done with so that they could both behave again like normal bedfellows and not, as he phrased it on one of his long therapeutic walks, 'like sexually deprived hypochondriacs.' That of course was part of the problem: Miriam had seized up entirely, and frankly, he thought, it was a bit unfair even if it was a bit painful for her. It wasn't as if they were both old fogies.

As the weeks went by he felt his own expansive nature tightening, becoming a nasty coil. He made every effort to counteract this. Indeed he thought his mistake had been to go too far in the direction of understanding. He would fan her when she was hot and rattle off some yarn when she showed signs of bursting into tears, as quite frequently happened when she dropped something or stood on the cat's tail or Susan sighed over her I Ching or Hanni swore at the complexities of the English language. He indulged her fetching up treats from the Austrian baker and telling her not to worry about her weight but to hack into the old applestrudel and the devil take the hormones. But he secretly resented it when she did gain weight.

One evening he snapped. From full flight before her moods, his own bucking at the sight of her hair so streelish and normally so rich like an auburn snake coiled around her head, and a crumb on her lip like a wart, he wheeled into counterattack. 'Pack it in, Miriam,' he snapped.

'Pack what in, Willy?' she said with that hurt look that was driving him mad.

'The whole shebang, Miriam,' he said. 'Pack it all in, you miserable old bag.'

'Mammy is not a bag,' piped up Susan, astonished at his tone. From his perch in the patio the Professor raised his nose from Schopenhauer and looked mildly amused.

'Think of Cambodia,' said Willy, floundering.

'What has Cambodia to do with it, Willy?'

'They're not worrying about their bloody hormones,' he said. 'Vitamins, Miriam! Vitamins!'

'I am not suffering from a lack of vitamins, Willy.'

'Ah, but the Cambodian women are, aren't they? But do we think of them? No, because we can't see farther than our own neurotic plumbing that's all bunged up because of excess, Miriam, excess! Peppermints and cream and liqueurs and let's try the Java this week, shall we, and applestrudel and oh dear, puff-puff, I'm dying, fan me, Willy, fan me, but divil the much else me, Willy, while the Paddys drink and the paddy fields rot and Cambodian women are dying on the run from maniac commies. Soon we'll have them over here along with our own maniacs and *then* we can sweat!'

Again he turned for respite towards the open sea. He walked as far as the lighthouse. A beautiful evening. The boats rocked going ding-dong like cow-bells. Old Ned lounged as usual waiting for the eels to bite. A woman was training an Alsatian to sit and wait. Nuns in pairs walked briskly along. How often had he painted it all? The ferry slid out with a great sigh bound for Holyhead. He had a mad urge to be on it, to escape.

Of course he cooled off, went back to applestrudel, *insisted* she treat herself, even bought her a string bag. He took her to the theatre, a farce, but she began to cry in the middle of it and they had to leave. In bed it was very trying. Miriam was like a rubber doll that squeaked if he pressed on it. When she wasn't drugged she was sweating. They who had slept like two large peas in a pod lay apart, sundered. He tried to keep far over to his own side and once, dreaming he was a hang-glider, fell out of the bed with a thump that shook the house. Then he could hardly sleep at all, went around with bags under his eyes, and his walks became nocturnal. He tried to jog but gave it up. Instead he walked for miles, often down to Killiney strand where on warm nights he would strip off and have a dip. He felt he was training in some discipline that hadn't yet been invented. Towards morning he might doze off for a couple of hours and then shamble down like a sleepy bear to his little art shop where Rose, his one assistant, worried over him. But how could he explain to a young kid? Bleakly he sat and gazed out on the pavement so blocked with cars now that women with prams were forced on to the street.

'What sort of a town are we becoming, Rose?' he would complain. 'A junk yard, that's what.' At night the bay that he liked to see as strings of diamonds on the brow of the land hurled its truth at him: congestion! A yacht sank in a storm. Only the tops of the mast stuck up from the water. He tried to paint it but gave up. The symbolism was oppressive. All was opaque adrift in currents of dirty green.

One night in bed he thought of his grandmother's yard, of milk churns in a row. That was exactly what he felt like, a churn full of nothing but a warm empty smell. And what did it matter now? Beside him Miriam, her mouth gaping, was already rehearsing the death rattle. And what a handsome, *balanced* woman she had been. How handsome she could still be . . . and as he thought this he fancied her eyes opened and she smiled at him. Her arm and bosom appeared to beckon and, as if touched by a benign spirit of the flesh he felt desire seeping through him in a healing draught. He reached out to touch her but she awoke, recoiled, brushing away his hand as if it were an insect. His mood changed to pique. He had a picture of his grandmother riding side-saddle through the clouds yelling at him. She had never liked Miriam, referred to her as a papist and a grocer's daughter, though later she was not averse to pocketing some of the grocer's loot for her old hacks. Artypants, she used to call Willy, scornful of all intellectuals. Now the crazy old woman shouted, 'Take her, Willy! Take her, you miserable old artypants!' as if she were a five-barred gate, and he rolled on Miriam, awkwardly, while she awoke fully now though drugged still and thinking it was another dream with him falling on her this time instead of the floor, resisting then through the shock of what he was up to but he was already purposeful, thrusting with little grunts of determination while she gasped for breath, squeaked, tried her elbows but then they were behind his neck and he was through the gap and there was nothing she could do but wait for him. He groaned and she thought he had finally arrived blowing like a whale but his will had snapped, the groan was directed at himself snagged on some point of disgust where desire had wilted to impotence.

'I'm sorry,' he said, rolling off her. The grandmother turned tail and galloped off in disgust. 'Did I hurt you?'

Miriam said nothing appearing to sink down beneath the clothes in a state of shock. Willy's anger flickered again. Would she make an issue of this now? What was it but a spot of honest lust. Happens in every marriage. And in these hard times? But he had always been so considerate, that was it. My sweet William, she used to say loving the way he caressed her. He lay glowing and sick as if he had jogged for a mile on a full stomach, and again wondered what it mattered now. He could grow fat and easy as an old eunuch, pace the bowling green with his cronies, play bridge, hide all the rest behind bright blue eyes and shag tobacco. He smoked a pipeful now vaguely wondering if there was any fruit juice in the fridge.

Miriam quietly left the bed. He heard her fetching something from the linen cupboard. The drawing room door closed quietly behind her. It was so unfair. How could she let rip after dropping a saucepan and not after this? They had at least always talked out their rows. It was like an insult, as if he had wilfully poured soup down her dress or spat on her shoe.

The next night Miriam made her bed in the utility room. The Professor and Susan exchanged glances. But it was only for a night. The next day she and Susan left for Bad Homburg to stay with her sister Constance who was married there. 'It will do me good to take the waters,' she said rather grandly to Hanni. Her skin looked dry and blotchy and Willy felt sorry for her but his mood was aloof. Their farewell was as casual as if she were going into town. A brief note on the kitchen table listed things to be done. They took a taxi to the airport. Overnight Willy, the Professor and Hanni were on their own.

For a few days the routine of the house carried on but it was like a clock that slowly ran down. When it finally stopped no one bothered to wind it again. A cheese fondue under Hanni's guidance was their last heroic effort together. Each took to foraging on his own. Slices of bread and half-empty tins lay about. Willy remonstrated but the two young people just shrugged. The Professor played his music and read. Hanni wrote endless letters to her swain, a cook in the Bernese Alps. Why she was there at all was a mystery to Willy. They had only taken her in in the hope that she would speak German with Susan. He had never heard them saying a word in that language and he was beginning to doubt that it was in fact Hanni's

mother tongue. Rhaeto-Romansch was probably more
her bag, he thought.

A spell descended on the house. Willy sat by the
window and read Poe. The throb of music from below
echoed the sinister heartbeat in the story. He watched the
tennis players in Clarinda Park. Had he capered about
like that once too?

One evening he roused himself from his torpor (and a
half-digested Chinese meal) and went down to the Professor's den. There the Professor and Hanni were propped
against the wall smoking. Books and records lay scattered
about. The air was heavy with a sweetness that caught
him in the throat. They giggled at him, high as the
Finsteraarhorn.

'Well,' he said to his son. 'What's it all about?' He
knocked a book aside with his toe.

'About?'

'Spinoza, Kant, the lot. What's the imperative sub
bloody specie aeternitatis?'

'Freedom's the trip, man,' said the youth, grinning up
at him foolishly.

'Is this freedom, you glib monster? Look at the mess.'

'Freedom's the trip, man,' repeated Hanni nodding her
large blond head like a puppet. Sadly Willy gazed upon
her. He really thought these mountainy Swiss shouldn't
attempt to live at sea level.

Then he was on his own. One morning the two went
off with rucksacks. Willy attacked the house as if it were
a hostile organism. When it was all done he sat down
feeling he had prepared rooms for an event that had been
called off. Beside him was his book on the Ottoman Turks
but he was at the point where Selim the Sot had come to
power. Inevitably he would want to strangle someone
with a bow string. Willy wandered down to the bowling
club. The green was loud with gaudy women in peaked
caps and he kept out of sight. Thrown back on himself he

sank into a kind of solipsism, and brooding on the word perceived its terrors. In the shop he wore an air of forlorn dignity that reminded Rose of her grandfather when he had one too many. But Willy had only one kidney and hardly indulged. A boil on his neck troubled him and he thought of Job. Miriam's letters were perfunctory. Susan had met a nice young man. They had even been to the casino. It might have been the correspondence of an aunt or friend killing a half-hour in a café. A card arrived from the Professor from Doolin. He was heading north and wanted more money. Eventually he reached Larne and crossed over to Scotland. Willy saw him trudging ever northward until he disappeared like a speck into the snows. Not a word from Hanni. She had gone to ground somewhere. Perhaps with her cook.

A fog descended on Dun Laoghaire. Voices were muffled. Cats rutted tirelessly in the park. Willy stalked them with the Professor's old air gun but took to his heels at a yelp of pain from a man's dog. 'Blackguards!' the man shouted. In his panic Willy threw away the gun. From the pier the fog horns were cries of animals doomed to extinction. Willy groaned aloud in sympathy. Lights hove into view, lanterns on a ghostly ship. People were wraiths. Then he realised that they were giving him a wide berth. 'Oooh!' he groaned louder. For the first time in his life he felt unwanted on his pier.

Walking down to Dalkey village he entered a pub where the works of local artists lined the walls. It was the dead hour of evening. Over a bitter lemon he sat and stared at his own latest contribution, a view of Bullock Harbour. Yet another. How many times had it tempted him back! The water was different or the boats, the sky, the people, and like a lover he would return to taste the new promise, and more often than not to sulk when it proved false. Or just pedestrian, as he considered the canvas in front of him. How many of his blithe flirtations with colour adorned the walls of middle-class homes around?

'It went last night, Mr. Featherstone,' said Seamus, polishing a glass.

'What?'

'Your picture.'

'Oh really?' said Willy. 'Do you know who bought it?'

'A young couple. They were sitting where you are now. Mind you, they only put a deposit down but they looked okay.'

Impulsively Willy asked for pen and paper stirred less by the sale of his picture than by a memory of Miriam and himself sitting here like that young couple planning their home. He wrote now of his loneliness, how much he missed her and Susan. He thought he even felt 'all steamed up' at times (no, it wasn't a cold, he had a bit of a boil but it wasn't too bad) as if over all that distance he occasionally picked up the signals of her distress (though he hoped she was feeling much better now). He went about life with a 'dogged determination' feeling at times very tired (he still slept badly), worried too by a feeling of 'chronic impotence' which saddened him because he knew how good they had been for each other in the past. He blamed himself. He had been impatient, inconsiderate and he hoped she would forgive him. He signed himself her 'sweet William'.

Willy slept well that night as if his spirit had found relief in a few words scribbled in a pub. In fact he rather enjoyed himself for the next few days. A neighbour's daughter—Lilly Buttons so called since her childhood habit of sewing on funny buttons on everything—sat for him and it was as if fortune smiled on his brush as well. Usually his portraits turned out rather literal. He had done one of Miriam and got his flesh tints wrong. She looked as if she was going to have a coronary. But now he scrumbled in his background with an abandon that strangely worked. He experienced that rare sensation of luck being on the painter's side. And the atmosphere in which he worked was bright. In the kitchen he relaxed with Lilly and her friend Bettina who amused them with outrageous poses. Bettina wanted to be painted too. And why not? There was possibly a vast reservoir of young women in Dun Laoghaire waiting to sit for him. He could attempt a nude. What he attempted in the kitchen was a dance, the Professor's music blaring through the house.

'How's Mrs. Featherstone?' asked Rose seeing him looking perky.

'Great form,' he said. 'Going to the casino. I only hope it's her own money she's losing.'

But a startling letter arrived from Miriam. She had waited to tell him her 'good news' until she was sure it was true. What was true? That she had become a 'new woman' no less. Constance had taken one look at her and brought her straight to her gynaecologist who had diagnosed acute oestrogen deficiency ('down to zero') and immediately put her on hormone replacement therapy (HRT) which was '*such* normal treatment for women here' that she couldn't understand why Dr. Foley hadn't suggested it. He, Willy, had been right after all (ha!), he was rather oldfashioned. She felt 'rejuvenated'. Her flushes had subsided, her skin was better, she was eating and sleeping better, she had lost weight and Dettlef saying she was looking *rassig*.

Willy immediately looked up the word and found it meant thoroughbred, racy, super, snazzy. Should he enter her in the Gold Cup?

Oestrogen, she informed him, was taken from mare's urine (or the National) 'which sounds awful, doesn't it, but that's the miracle of science for you.' But it saddened her to hear that her 'own sweet William' was so down in the dumps. He was not to worry about a thing. Wait until she came home, 'and that will be soon, darling,' and all his little worries would disappear, also his impotence (*impotence?*) which was bound to be secondary and natural in a man of his age 'though I'm not of course saying that you're old, Willy dear, to me you'll always be young' (good grief). She would show him that she could deal with the matter 'quite adequately' (it sounded as if he had a bed wetting problem). She was partly to blame because of her condition. The doctor told her she had been suffering from . . . and here Willy couldn't decipher the word . . . dysparumsa? but HRT (sounded like a slick young executive) would have taken care of that too by now. As to his other problems she had met a 'darling little man' called Herr Schmitz at the baths. He was a 'walking encyclopaedia of cures' especially the old ones. He swore by stewed onions as a cure for insomnia. How was his boil? He should treat it with tincture of iodine. And, incidentally, Herr Schmitz said he had been impotent for five years and 'then it went away just like that' (perhaps he had sampled the local twitch) 'so you are not to *worry*, darling.'

Willy threw the letter aside. He hated born-again women. They ended up wearing wigs and having their faces lifted. They flaunted their health and well-being as a Cause. He hated women with Causes. Miriam, he feared, would get endless mileage out of HRT with the bridge and bowling brigade, the BBBs. And was his putative impotence the talk of Bad Homburg spa?

A great wind came up from the north-east bringing with it the first bite of autumn. The pier was deserted. Leaves whirled about the tennis courts. A grey sea foamed at the mouth. Even the one-eyed terrier next door snapped more convincingly at the heels of passers-by. Willy sat by the window, Selim the Sot still waiting plumply on his knee like a malevolent child.

Hanni and the Professor reappeared out of nowhere.

They had met by chance on the way home. The old pattern set in. Willy's flatulence turned to palpitations.

When Miriam sailed into the shop he didn't recognise her at first. She had slimmed all right but as if someone had taken bits out of her at random. Her upper teeth appeared larger as if they were slowly engulfing her chin. And what was that sticking out of her hair? Good grief, it *was* her hair! Cut away, mutilated, her splendid locks.

'How do you like me?' she said making her dress swirl around.

Willy thought for a moment and said, 'Snazzy I think would be the word.'

That night he began a study of Ghengis Khan. Miriam flounced about chattering like a parakeet. She preened in a new peignoir that gave her the look of a ravaged old whore. When she slipped in beside him they lay for a while in silence. He waited for some part of her to touch him. When it did (her toes seeking coyly to engage his) he turned to her with a stoney expression and said, 'Miriam, I fear it's not secondary but quite definitely primary.'

What on earth are you talking about?'

'My dingdoorum.'

'Oh my poor sweet Willy . . .'

'We must be brave about it.'

'Can't we try?'

'*Try*, woman?' he breathed fixing her with a ferocious eye. 'Can you *try* to drive an old jaloppy that won't start?'

As the days passed he convinced himself, with a mixture of relief and consternation, that he had spoken the truth. Impotence lay like lead in his veins. Miriam couldn't do enough for him. He never had it so good. She fetched him up jars of his favourite honey from the delicatessen. He put on weight but it was 'good, Willy,' she said, 'good, you need plenty of strength.' She bought him a new reel for his rod. She would have bought him a new dingaling if it could be installed. But there was no horse piss for the knackered male, he thought, ruefully and with a little pride.

And it was quite trying in bed. He endeavoured to keep to his own side but now she was much lighter and rolled after him—or it *appeared* as if the force of gravity were to blame. In fact if she thought he were in the least favourably disposed she edged over to poke and finger him as if he suffered from some kind of itch. His palpitations grew worse. He began to sweat and had to change his pyjamas. Once he got up quietly and made his bed in the utility room.

He didn't stay there of course. It was just a warning to her to cool it.

Plato and Passion

When I hear of people having a 'Platonic relationship' I think of my Aunt Adelaide and the passion she put into hers. I fancy I was the only person who knew it was a passion, and the way I found out was pure accident. In my first year as a student in Cork I lodged with Adelaide and Uncle Jimmy and in that time I was keeping up a wildly romantic correspondence with a girl in Dublin. We never got around to marrying each other afterwards but I should say we both profited from a very fine apprenticeship in writing love letters. Some of mine were so beautiful I kept the original drafts, and coming upon one such the other day in a pile of old papers I damn near wept. How one brimmed at seventeen with expectation! A chivalrous time still, one managed to convey one's great ambition to plunge into the sexual bush while yet beating around it for pages at a time. I pined her presence to feel, her body to behold, her eyes to gaze into, her laugh to hear, her supple waist to encircle in the dance, the *gap in her front teeth* to dwell on! Catch me dwelling on a gap in her teeth front or back when I had her up the Furry Glen!

My great problem at the time, however, was in hiding this correspondence from the vulgar gaze. I wasn't worried about Adelaide and Jimmy but their son Ron was a menace. He was a pimply envious wretch who has since become a Special Branch detective, bearing out my worst suspicions of him then. He was for ever putting stuff on his face and wiping it off with *my* face cloth. I also suspected him of wiping his oily comb on my towel and of using my shaving brush. So rather than leave the letters anywhere in my room where he was undoubtedly snooping, I tucked them away cute as hell in a corner of a rarely opened press containing spare blankets and the like. It was when my fingers were groping for them one day that I discovered another packet of letters loosely tied with a blue ribbon. About ten in all, they were addressed to Adelaide from a man called John. I peeked at a few (in the interests of comparative technique) but they seemed pretty tame stuff, all about having enjoyed their walk together, or the meal or the film together and looking forward to meeting again soon, your fond friend, John. If the spark of passion had ignited between them it fizzled out well and truly in the ink.

It came as something of a shock then one day when, with the house to ourselves, those same letters became the subject of a delicate tête à tête between Adelaide and myself. I had noticed a subtle change in her attitude towards me of late, a silence almost which I interpreted as disapproving. My late nights and general lack of concentration were not a good example to the budding detective. So I was immediately on the defensive when she said out of the blue, 'I wanted to talk to you about those letters.'

'Letters?' I said blandly but felt the blood rush to my cheeks.

'The ones in the press.' Her face was grave as she stood by the cooker waiting for the kettle to boil. 'You've seen them. haven't you?'

'Yes, I did see them,' I admitted at once. 'But believe me, Auntie. I don't read other people's letters.'

She said nothing to this for a while because of course she knew better. I didn't think she was capable of acquiescing even in a small lie. But it was clear at once that for her it was no small matter.

'Sit down,' she said. 'We'll have a cup of tea.'

'You don't believe me?'

'Sit down like a good boy.' I sat down meekly, watching her prepare the tea. 'I want to tell you something,' she said when she had settled herself. 'Those letters were written to me by a man who is very dear to me.'

'Auntie, you must believe me, I couldn't help finding them.'

'Precisely.' She smiled sadly. 'And I'm sure you're wondering why they were hidden away like that.'

'Why should I? I also had hidden away my letters.'

'Ah, but your letters are, I am sure, *different* from mine.'

I felt myself blushing all over again. My God, what had I missed? Had passion erupted in letter four or five? Was it so intense by letter ten that it had to be muffled by a lot of old blankets?

'How different?' I said, gamely trying to be man of the world about it but slopping tea into the saucer. After all, it was none of my business if Adelaide was still lusting shamelessly after some lost lover. Looking into her round placid features (now rather florid) I tried to visualise her in a shameless posture but felt embarrassed.

'You saw when those letters were written?'

'No.'

'I'm sure you did,' she said evenly. 'It was during the war when Uncle Jimmy was still in the Signal Corps and I was in London. Ron was four at the time.'

I realised with a sudden thrill of relief that I had got it all wrong. Aunt Adelaide, that most fervent Catholic woman, feared *my* disapproval, *my* disillusionment and shock at having discovered her—albeit very much *post flagrante delicto*—in adultery!

My cup steadied. I was prepared to be magnanimous. After all, I knew what passions were and how one had to conceal them. I was confident she could even tell Jimmy about it. He was a big lovable man who snoozed all day on a chair in the museum and just about managed to get through the *Evening Echo* at night. If his wife was still lusting he surely had only himself to blame.

As I listened to Adelaide recount the circumstances of her meetings with John, however, I found I was still very wide of the mark. My first impressions of the letters had been right. Far from being the passionate affair I imagined in cheap hotels and shady parks it seemed a most harmless series of encounters.

John had been her boss then, a man of thirty-five, a devout Catholic like herself, married with three children and 'devoted to his family as I was to mine'. They met and talked, had meals together, went for long walks and . . . they knew.

'We knew,' she said, looking at me with her beautiful soft grey eyes. 'You understand?'

Had Henry James been eavesdropping in the hall he might have understood, but I didn't, I only knew one thing about passions and that was that I wanted to indulge them, terminating as quickly as possible my virginal state.

'Understand what?' I said impatiently now. I had a lecture and anyway it was all a bit of a bore.

'We knew,' Adelaide merely repeated, nodding her head.

Thus ended on a mysterious note what would have gladdened the heart of Henry James—Adelaide's first instalment of her revelations to me. These continued at intervals until her death and gradually became part of my own life and an essential part of the bond between us. But on that first day I left for my lecture feeling I had been cajoled into saying lines in a very boring and esoteric play to which Adelaide's admonition to me on parting that this was now 'our secret' was like an idiotic curtain

line. As I made my way up the college walk I decided she
was sexually and emotionally deprived and if Jimmy
didn't pull his socks up—or whatever the erotic equiva-
lent was in his somnolent world—he would be reading all
about it some afternoon in the *Echo*.

Summer holidays came around and in the rough and
tumble of earning money in a London canning factory I
forgot all about Adelaide's mysterious liaison. One
punchdrunk night I even managed to sing the *Sash* and
lose my virginity, in that order, with a wee thing from
Belfast, forging then what I still consider to be the only
sensible solution to the Northern Problem. On my return
in the autumn I sported a new tweed jacket and a calm
maturity. This was so strong I offended the college's
moral guardians by moving into a flat with two others
(flats were dens of iniquity!) and intended visiting Adelaide and Jimmy and all my other Cork relatives only on
the rarest family occasions.

Scarcely had a week of the new term elapsed, however,
when a card from Adelaide arrived at college, addressed
to the English Literature Society, of which I was now
auditor. She hoped I would have lunch with her the
following week, naming the place and the hour. For the
benefit of my friends I groaned aloud (as auditor I was
continually groaning aloud at everything) but naturally
I accepted. At least she had picked the Oyster Tavern, a
decent place where a fellow could have a drink or two
while ordering from huge menus.

To my surprise our meal turned out to be very pleasant,
mainly because Adelaide allowed me to monopolise the
conversation. She was sprightly indeed and looked elegant in a new mauve costume. We traded family news
and I amused her with a laundered account of my London
exploits, savouring that sense of power I thought I had
discovered over events and people. Adelaide's invitation,
after all, was but further proof of this. No mention was

made of 'our secret' but it loomed in the background, and from the subtle turn she gave to the conversation at one point I knew her main purpose in meeting me was to reaffirm her faith in my discretion.

'An intimate place this,' she said, looking around from our corner table. 'But then this is a very intimate city.'

'An exalted village,' I agreed, pouring myself another boring provincial Guinness.

'They want to know all about you.'

'Oh, benighted, girl, benighted.'

'Yes,' she said, giving me that calm but slightly pleading look I had come to expect. 'But at least in a village you know who your friends are.'

'Ah!'

My sense of power received another fillip when on parting she slipped a ten shilling note into my hand. Hush money? For her Platonic peccadilloes? I accepted, disdaining to bother myself too much with her motives. Quite clearly it was a hang-up of some kind and the best thing was to humour her. She quickly arranged another lunch, with a swirl of comment about how good it had done her to get out of the house, how impossible it was to get Jimmy to go anywhere with her and Ron was still a dope. With this last especially I heartily agreed.

Having lunch with Adelaide thus became a regular event the remaining three years of my student life. I marvel now at how patiently and subtly she allowed me to hold court, to *impress* her, even encouraging me to show her my poetry, while luring me ever deeper into the dim regions of her attachments to this man's memory. That they were dim and possibly, deranged I had no doubt, yet within months she had contrived so naturally to bring 'our secret' into the open between us that to have divulged it would have seemed like selfbetrayal. From the day she slipped a mention of 'my beloved' into some rambling story about the war and I (psychoanalysing her at the time) said by way of clarification, 'You mean John?' my fate was sealed. I had truly become her confidant.

Pursuing the archetypal source (I was full of Jung at the time) of Adelaide's suspected neurosis was indeed my greatest mistake, for thereafter I found it impossible to extricate myself. From being privy to what I concluded was the unrequited puppy love of a middleaged woman I found myself tacitly conniving at it, my connivance often being secured before I knew what was happening. In all her convictions (and prejudices) Adelaide typified the good Catholic wife and mother and *any* suggestion to the contrary seemed ludicrous, yet when he surfaced again and again in remarks so casual as to be fleeting, I realised how ever-present 'my beloved' was in her thoughts. She would complain about Jimmy's absent-mindedness. Army men were supposed to be sticklers for order but Jimmy had become so used to having an orderly following him around that he was continually forgetting to close things or even to switch off the wireless or the electric fire. But then 'my beloved's uncle' used to be a bit like that, also an army man. When conversation touched on people's ability to memorise she revealed that she had a mental picture of every comma and full-stop in 'the letters'. And when the efficacy of prayer came up, 'my beloved's favourite prayer' was quickly slipped in by way of reference. It is a measure of how I had come to focus on these references that I entered this short prayer—'God give me the sincerity to accept the things I cannot change, the courage to change the things I can and the wisdom to know the difference'—into the journal I was keeping. Like a shadowy stage manager John spoke but infrequently, but when he did the whole drift and balance of the play seemed to rest on his words.

I tackled her, of course, on a few occasions. I was old enough to know that this dream of perfect love with John was too good to be true. How long would it have stood up to the abrasions of family life? Would he be any different from Jimmy (or any other husband) now? After a few months indeed John had moved with his family to the midlands and their correspondence ceased. Wasn't that sufficient proof that it had all been but a nice friendship? When she discovered after the war that he had emigrated to Australia, was there any point in preserving his memory as something so precious?

I had the feeling that Adelaide had been waiting for these questions because she seemed very glad when I asked them. It was as if I had queried the genuineness of her pearls and she was able to admit that, no, indeed they were quite common, she possessed nothing extraordinary at all.

'It was never a dream,' she said simply. 'We were both too mature for that. Also there was a war on and no one had time for dreams. No, it was more a question of degree.'

'Degree of what?'

'Of knowing.'

'Ah . . . knowing what?'

'Knowing that had we been able under God to consummate our love our cup would have been as full of life's bitterness as anyone's, but it would have been full. Always. That is the difference.'

'How could you have known?'

'We *knew*.'

As an enthusiastic handballer, I had come to hear in those two words the smack of the winning butt, the ball rolling back irretrievably from the base of the high and mighty front wall. Easier to scale it than win the match.

The physical aspect of the whole Platonic affair intrigued me for its theological niceties but I was too unsure of myself then to broach it. What went on behind Adelaide's doe-like eyes when she thought of John was for me *terra incognita*. To enquire would have been like asking one's mum. A few years later, however, considerably better informed about the older age brackets and indeed not a little cocksure of myself, I was less reticent. I hadn't met Adelaide or seen my old haunts for about five years and, being happy at the time, my reunion with them was a joyous occasion. I returned as to a stage on which I had performed creditably in a comedy of youthful errors. Forgotten were the humiliations, the near despair at times at one's ignorance and inexperience. At *our* table in the Tavern I stood Adelaide the best lunch she ever had and along the way was delighted to discover that 'my beloved' was alive and well and active as ever in the wings. Indeed it was all too obvious she had been looking forward to giving him an outing for old times' sake.

'You're an old flirt, you know, Adelaide,' I ventured in my best suave manner, pouring more wine. She was flushed and a trifle skittish. I felt the moment had come.

'My mother used to say,' she recalled between titters, 'that there should be a bit of a flirt in every woman and a bit of a fool in every man.'

'Within reason, of course.'

'Of course.'

'Ah, but you have refined the game,' I said, clinking my glass against hers, 'to a fine art.'

'What do you mean?'

'All these years lying in the arms of Jimmy while dreaming of John.'

Colour drained from her cheeks and then shot up again. Whatever nerve I had touched it was very real. A sense of the power I used to have over her kindled in me but now her lovely eyes held no sad plea, rather hurt disbelief. When she spoke her voice shook slightly.

'I would never have thought,' she said, 'after all you know . . .'

'But that's just it, my dear aunt, I know nothing!'

'. . . after all you know that you would suspect me of fickleness.'

'Not fickleness, Adelaide,' I said, roused. 'Sin. Vicarious adultery.' If I had struck her she couldn't have looked more shocked. Her cheeks received another instant blood rinse. 'Isn't there something about coveting one's neighbour's spouse?' I added.

She sat for a moment in stunned silence but then her expression went through the most elusive change to one of genuine astonishment. If she was an actress she was a damn good one.

'I'm amazed at you,' she said at last.

'Are you?'

'I truly am. Covet? Me, is it? I don't think I'd be capable of coveting another man.'

'What?!' I gaped at her. 'Sure you're at it all the time girl! You thought of him endlessly.'

'I *thought* of him. Ah, but that's *different.*'

Instantly I was back with her in the kitchen, a scrawny youth hiding love letters, discovering hers. We had come full circle.

'How?' I asked as bluntly as then. 'Did you keep him locked up in a mental bottle like a djinn?'

Now she relaxed, smiling at me with a kind of forgiveness. She was very calm again though her skin looked taut and waxen. Clearly she had concluded that I was still too young to understand, so she lectured me quietly, even replenishing my glass in case I got bored.

'Do you still practise your religion?' she asked.

'Yes,' I lied.

'Well, then you must know that we communicate with God directly through the sacraments and indirectly through our love for each other. We are all part of the Mystical Body of Christ. Sometimes He makes it easier for us by creating great love between us. Other times our cup is not so full, there are others with whom we would clearly be happier, much happier. We know this and there is no use denying it. I have always thought of John as a man God placed before me in His wisdom, a man with whom by His grace I knew I could have shared my life more fully, infinitely more fully, than with any other but from whom by the same bountiful grace I had to part. But could I have denied that I loved him? I still do, to say otherwise would be really to sin, to lie. But I don't have to examine the nature of that love. Inevitably it has remained spiritual.' She smiled now more fully, inclining her head towards me. 'I assure you I never had to put him into a bottle, no more than I had to shut Jimmy or Ron out from my love. I have been a faithful and devoted wife and mother, I am not afraid to say it. Jimmy and Ron have been for me a full part of the sacrament of marriage. John was merely part of the sacrifice that went into its fulfilment but as such an essential part. But I could no more confuse the two than I could confuse good and evil.'

My head was spinning. I sat back and looked at her, lost in admiration.

Later I raged. She put the whole rigmarole into a long letter and I fumed, kicking chairs, shouting 'Semantics!' to the wall. My feelings about her had become utterly divided. One half of me was lovingly and understandingly involved; my youth, after all, had been spent in the company of 'my beloved'. But the other half refused to have anything to do with her spiritual bag of tricks. I still believed it was all an unhealthy and significant obsession, a quasi-religious veil hiding a very real but suppressed need to act or create or truly love or get out and live, yes *live!* I also saw in it the urge to inflict pain on herself as though in retribution for not having lived, for having spent her years in a kind of sacramental limbo, masochism under the guise of religious sacrifice. Eventually I saw in it a 'repressed nun syndrome'. She realised soon after marrying lazy Jimmy that she had made a mistake, that she really had a vocation, so she raised a casual friendship to pristine and sacrificial heights. John is really God with whom she can be as virginal and ecstatic as any cloistered nun. No wonder she took offence when I accused her of vicarious adultery! What nun wouldn't be shocked if accused of entertaining carnal thoughts while contemplating the Cross?

Again a long interval elapsed in which our letters became general and infrequent. I had other things to worry about. There came a time when I was no longer so happy, when love lay about me like debris. Life slipped and rattled under every step I took. If I ever thought of Adelaide and her beloved during that period it was with wry reflections on all idealised relationships. In the world one dealt with broken things.

Then Jimmy died while I was flat on my back with rheumatic fever and about a year later Adelaide contributed a new and perhaps the most significant chapter to her love story. In a letter she described how one morning she was washing up as usual when she was overcome by a most extraordinary feeling. It was 'as intense as pain but not pain,' rather as if all her 'nerves and energies and instincts had become concentrated and then uprooted,' as if her 'very insides had been pulled up by the roots.' When she recovered she felt convinced that something terrible had happened and her first thoughts went to 'my beloved'. She was going to put an advertisement in the Australian papers in an effort to locate him.

For the first time it occurred to me that my aunt was probably psychic. I hated to think she was actually insane.

What comes now will read like a happy ending. Adelaide found her beloved, or at least she found his wife . . . in Adelaide (oh, no!). John was dead and . . . yes, he had been on his deathbed about the time Adelaide was having her insides uprooted.

Whoever said people had stopped telling ghost stories? Now a touching sequel.

Adelaide went to Adelaide and was received most cordially by John's widow. If John had ever spoken of her I shall never know. Adelaide said she was looking up long-lost friends in Australia and it was natural for her to come and pay her last respects. She laid a big bunch of red roses on John's grave and wrote me a letter full of heartfelt thanks for my 'understanding and love,' saying that whatever misunderstandings there had been she loved and was proud of me for one thing: I had kept 'our secret'. How did she know? In Cork everything comes back to you, however small.

At the risk of being blacked for the rest of my life by the Special Branch (do they read short stories?) I have divulged 'our secret' here for what it's worth. Adelaide's remaining wish that she be reunited with her beloved John was granted—or not—a few months ago. If it was, poor Jimmy will still be out in the cold, but perhaps he will be more content to loll about on some cloud and discuss the heavenly news with other indolent beings. Ecstasy in any form was not for him. At Adelaide's graveside I thought of the two famous lines from Donne's poem:

> *Love's mysteries in souls do grow*
> *But yet the body is his book.*

—The body, Mr. Plato?

—But of course, sir! It's all a very good idea really.

Heat

Under its grid the cobalt's luminous energy appeared to rise up and enter his blood, chilling him with a power as cold and distant as the stars. Mick O'Dwyer had beckoned him in to the sterilising room as he passed by, and there it was beneath his feet in its bed of water like some creature of the deep frozen forever in the blue gleam of its signal. So silent was it among the boxes of syringes, so far from the rap and roar of the factory, that Danny had a picture of them, Mick and himself, as insiders, people who had slipped behind the wheel and din of life and stood now, alert and still, in the eye of its monstrous power.

What would happen if he fell in? 'Not much,' Mick had said, adding with a smile, 'if you didn't swim around for too long.' And now in the dark bedroom Danny saw himself diving into the blue pool as into the true element of his spirit that had remained hidden from him, locked away as though he had no right or competence to enter it, diving down and then rising to shiver into being again like a character in Dr. Who, to stand at the window alive with the cobalt's ghostly light, the kids below running screaming into their homes. But the colour changed to the dirty copper flowing from the first spluttering hose they had trained on the fire.

He thought: I should have let it burn, the factory, instead of sounding the alarm and grabbing the extinguisher. The small tongues of flame were darting greedily among the broken cartons. In a minute the stacks of cardboard boxes would have gone up. The breeze whistling through the open warehouse doors would have carried the flame into the factory itself, engulfing the partitions and causing the bags of polypropylene to melt and fuse. People would have thrown down their earphones and run for the exits. But he had rushed for the alarm shouting 'Fire! Fire!' and later, standing hot and embarrassed in the assembly room while Mr. Gully commended him for his swift action, Danny realised that even as his hand had reached for the small hammer to break the glass of the alarm he had been moved by the presence of the cobalt, moved almost in a religious way as if, only a few minutes earlier, he had been allowed a peep into the tabernacle of power, and now the factory was no longer just walls and a roof and lines of machinery but a precious edifice built around a magic stone.

The thought mocked him while he listened to Mr. Gully uttering grim warnings about smoking on the premises. He felt tricked by the righteous words, the slick bull-necked tirade that masked a dumb ritual, no less than he had been deceived by the mysterious veil of blue masking a dumb isotope harnessed to a gauge. Once before Mr. Gully had praised him openly for the tidiness of his work place. Across from him stood Smithy and Donaldson with smirks on them. And there was Dympna in the front row smiling and pleased as punch. Her fella. Man of the hour.

In the street below boys played at commandos shooting from the unlit hallways. The power had failed after tea and it was a novelty with only candles and lamps flickering in the houses. His mother had brought him up a candle but he had blown it out.

He thought of Dympna, their walk (was the pier in darkness too?), their two drinks in Walters. His body tensed as if preparing for another ordeal. She would be tender in the shadow of the pier wall. Later, on one of the red stools in the lounge she would sit erect with her knees together and sip her vodka and lime. They prided themselves on not being part of the singalong mob. But there were limits to individuality. 'Thirty quid!' she had exclaimed when he said he had signed on for a philosophy course. The card he had picked up in a pub was soiled and wrinkled. She held it by a corner as if afraid of contamination. 'Probably a rip-off,' she said. 'What's it all for anyway?'

And that was the point, because he had expected to be told all about philosophy, to dip into the wisdom of ages, whereas the tutor only dwelt on how the mind worked, what parts of it take over at certain times, what happens when we daydream or lose ourselves in anger. He made them do exercises sitting very still, just taking in what they saw and heard without thinking too much about it, being aware of themselves, the weight of the body on the chair, the clothes on the body, seeing and hearing at the same time what was within and without but with no immediate search for 'meaning'.

Meaning, Danny had thought, was what it was all about. Still it was important to him to be there between a housewife and a young farmer who said he had come to the course because he was bored with pulling cabbages. Hadn't he come for the same reason? And the farmer was out in the fields all day not stuck behind a machine!

'But where does it get you?' Dympna went on. 'Isn't it only aping the college boys?' She believed in focusing attention on what was within range. Danny was a bit of a dreamer, 'as soft as an egg inside but as complicated,' as she expressed it to his sister. It was what had attracted her to him—their first night out he never once mentioned football or discos—but was also, she soon realised, the fatal chink in her knight's armour. Or rather, the armour

of his job and life that should be bearing down on the
obstacles in his path was proving to have a thousand
chinks through each of which Danny was tempted to
peep, ambition meanwhile whistling past his ears. At
twenty-six it was a bit late for dreaming.

'Truth waits in us all,' the tutor told the group. 'And
it is now we have to reach for it, not yesterday which has
passed or tomorrow which may never come. We are all
intellectuals.' He even rhymed it, saying, 'We can fly to
knowledge without ever going to college.' Danny regret-
ted not having had that on his tongue when Dympna
came out with her sneer about the college boys. Still, if
she had asked, 'What *is* this knowledge?' he would have
had no answer. He had ceased to talk about it. They went
for their walks and discussed other things. But it upset
him that he had started a search which she showed no
desire to share. As a creature awakens from some state of
instinct to a canny awareness of itself as a solitary being,
he was asking himself the crucial question: Why Dympna?
Why not another? Why anyone right now? He was growing away from her, from their cosy plans, their account
with the Dublin Savings Bank (target: £1000 down for
the mortgage, saving £20 a week), their budgeted two
drinks in Walters, a few more on a Saturday night.

A lorry roared by and shook the house. He hoped the
power failure would last. In the lull of traffic that followed,
his father's voice below took up the receding hum. The
candlelight had played on his face as on an image graven
and timeless. Through half-closed eyes Danny had flipped
in a time loop in which *he* was his father as a young man
looking out upon life from a kitchen full of the same
sounds and shadows, a place disturbed only by human
thought and sinew. He would have sat before such a man
with features full of strong resignation, burlier perhaps
(to judge by an old photo of his grandfather) with fiery

whiskers, telling of his action, proudly repeating Mr. Gully's words.

'What . . . do . . . you . . . think . . . is . . . at . . . stake?' Mr. Gully had spaced his words with dramatic effect. 'Two hundred jobs and one fag end, that's what's at stake. If it hadn't been for the swift action of Danny McGee here . . .' At the end, after preaching his favourite gospel of cleanliness in toilet, canteen and locker room ('We have a party of visitors today and I was appalled at the matches and papers strewn about'), he reverted to jobs, all jobs, 'in these times of want and insecurity' calling them 'gold, pure gold.'

Danny sat at his machine, numbed and empty, grateful only that with the noise there was no need for him to speak to anyone. If 'truth', he thought savagely, as the tutor said, was the quarry, then what he had been praised for was mere chance.

The syringes travelled up the elevator from the hopper and into the drums where they were vibrated around with a great noise until finally dropping into their polythene bags. Occasionally they bunched in the rails and seemed to quiver with impatience until he freed them. Thus at times he had waited, quivering, to be off work to meet Dympna. Down the line more product was moving, vibrating, dropping. Nimble fingers were scooping up the bags from the conveyor and putting them into cartons. Blue ear phones, yellow (Dympna's were yellow with a black stripe), red, each mind a hush and hiss and a hum and again a hush and a hiss, and scratchy voices from far away. One came to him from over his shoulder.

'What's your . . .?' It belonged to one of the party of American Chinese visiting the plant. Danny turned and shook his head. 'No speak American chink,' he said with his lips. 'Fuck off.' The visitor beamed and repeated his question, putting his mouth close to Danny's ear. His breath was sweet and heavy from wine.

'What's your hourly rate?'

'About 80,000,' Danny shouted. He provided other facts. A dud syringe was blown out by the air jet and struck the little man in the face. Great fun. The slit of his eyes sealed up in a smile.

'Good,' he said, patting Danny on the shoulder and trotting after the group. Danny did not look in Dympna's direction but he knew that she was watching him. She liked to see him talking to people, being involved. At such moments he hated her most. She loved to guide his nose into some close and smelly conceit of himself. As if one day he could believe in it and turn it into something strong and fine. He shouldn't be such a loner, she urged. Even in the canteen she noticed him frequently sitting apart from the others (what *he* had noticed on his first day was that the women all tended to crowd together in one corner) or joking with the men he had worked with in dispatch before being trained as an 'operative' complete with white coat and ear phones. He should be sitting with the technicians and fitters and learning from them, learning perhaps about the huge injection moulders to which he might move on. Her own brother Dan had started in his kind of job ('Routine really, just knowing how to service your machine, isn't that right?') before going on to become an electrician.

What Danny could not explain was that he was losing his feel for the simplest forms of communication. When he sat with his old mates from dispatch he would hang on their words as if searching for clues to the sense of normal human fellowship he had once enjoyed. Often in the canteen he experienced rather than heard the noise, the bursts of laughter, break around him, and then he was afraid to utter the simplest words and attended to those of others as if he were a foreigner in his own country picking up the idiom and slang of his fellow workers. Or he would be tempted to say too much, words would spill from him, a story badly told or what his brother was up to. He might lose the thread entirely or bungle the point, and then his mates (especially Smithy) would look at him as if indeed he was a foreigner trying to get his tongue around the language.

One evening, reading a library book about a man who studied ducks and lived with them, Danny startled his mother by saying that she had been 'imprinted' on him. He elaborated. The idea seemed to explain a lot. He argued that he — and maybe all working class people — had never learned to think at all but had the thoughts of the higher-ups, the experts and poshies, imprinted on them. They had been fed with ideas about themselves as he fed his machine with syringes. Then through the door he heard his mother wondering aloud to his father whether 'knocking about with that communist Billy Caffrey' was good for him. Perhaps Father Nolan should have a word.   Disgusted, Danny took to wearing ear phones in the home. He took down from the wall the photo of him that had appeared in a company brochure looking resplendently white and clean and efficient at his machine. His father drew aside and said, 'Look, son, if the job is getting you down, all that noise and everything, well, look for something else. Maybe what you need to do is get out in the open. I heard from Matt Twomey there may be a job going up in Larkin's yard . . .' Which of course started a row with Dympna who thought that his father's concern would simply turn him back into a labourer. What he needed was 'to cop himself on' and not go around pretending he was 'a bloody genius or something.'

Danny ignored them. He bought a diary and wrote down what he saw. In the mornings before work he recorded his dreams. On their walks he would talk about them and Dympna listened, suppressing her impatience. 'Real' thought appeared to him in one dream as a dark shambling thing lagging far behind on the road where his body raced along. He hadn't lost his head—at least when he put his hand up to touch it it was still there—but it was manned only by the everyday brain maintaining essential services like feet and elbows, breathing and bowel movements. The shape wasn't something threatening, some horror in the subconscious waiting to pounce. When he tried to will it as such slowing down, tempting it to overtake, it hid behind a tree like a shy monster. And the next morning it still followed him around the factory! (At this point Dympna suggested he should take a week's holiday). He felt it lurking in places, waiting to uncoil like a Jack-in-the-box from every carton of product he slit open.

When he did take a week off the sun blazed as if, in league with the others, it approved of his getting out and away from his obsessions. He messed about with his brother's skiff and went for rides through the Wicklow hills on his old Honda. His favourite place became a narrow grassy ledge high up on the Scalp. There he sat and scribbled things in his diary. He tried to express what he felt but the words fell dry and lifeless like dust upon the page.

He even made a list of other jobs he could take up. Lighthouse keeper was one that appealed but on enquiry he found that he was over-age and under-educated. There was forestry work but again his background was unsatisfactory and anyway he couldn't tell one tree from the next.

'You are trees,' he said, lying on his back and addressing the greenery above his head. 'Hello, trees.' He patted the warm rock beside him. 'Hello, rock. We both crazy things.' In large letters he wrote down: IM GOING CRAZY ON THE SCALP. This was a great joke and he hooted with laughter. For a while he seriously considered taking out his share of the money from the bank and just

bumming around the place . But what would that solve?
When he stood up things went black for a moment and
he had the sensation of falling through space. Shaken, he
lost his nerve for the descent and climbed over the ridge
and down by the golf course and the artificial ski slope.
Sitting in the plush lounge of the hotel he imagined that
the set of clubs beside him were his. He started an eye
flirt with a young barmaid and she and her mates began
to giggle at him. Then he was back at his machine again
and everyone was saying what a lovely tan he had, as if
he'd been abroad.

'Jimmy!' a woman called in the street below. 'You
come in here this minute, you young pup!'

All around in the dark street people were waiting for
the light to come on, their voices hushed. Danny had a
picture of caves and then of molten steel bursting like
gold from a gap in the wall and flowing among the streets,
the people emerging from the houses to stand and gaze
at it, their faces bright and glowing. In the factory the
syringes were golden pens dropping into silver bags and
he scooped them up, scattering them among the children.

In the afternoon he had sat lost in thought ('circling
thoughts', the tutor would have said) and when he looked
up it was to see Smithy leafing through the diary he had
placed beside him on the table. 'What's this?' he read
aloud. 'I'm twenty-six and know nothing. But I'm a good
robot. That's one truth.' For a few seconds, his heart
pounding, Danny held back, hoping that Smithy would
toss the book back on the table. But with a triumphant
glance at the others, he read on: 'Walters—all the men
staring at the box like at mass waiting for the consecra-
tion.' Then: 'I'm going crazy on the Scalp.' Amid laughter
Smithy said, 'That's a queer fuckin' place to be going
crazy.' Danny reached across and tried to snatch the
book but Smithy jerked it up. A chair was upturned and
then the table as Danny lunged. Smithy caught him with

a side swipe that sent him flying and Danny reached for
a chair but when he swung it around it connected with
the phones on the wall beside him. By order of the
management the numbers on them had been removed to
discourage incoming calls, and now as if something had
popped in Danny's brain, this became the real object of
his fury. 'As if we were bloody nameless creatures,' he
cried, striking at them again. Ignoring Smithy entirely he
turned towards where the buns were displayed in a
vending machine as though intent on settling a score with
them, and perhaps with the awful soup dispensers as
well . . . . And there was Mr. Gully in the doorway,
staring in astonishment at his golden boy.

'I suppose in one sense it's quite an achievement,' he
said later in his office. Danny stood before him, pale and
tight-lipped. 'In the morning I commend you for saving
the factory from being burnt down, in the afternoon I
have to reprimand you for trying to wreck it with a chair.
What was it all about?'

'A personal matter.'

'Personal matters are to be dealt with after work, is
that clear?'

The door-bell rang. That would be Dympna. Danny
got up and lit the candle. What would he tell her about
the fight? The truth? That suddenly appeared enormous,
entirely outside their world. But he saw that she would
approve of his action as she understood it. The kind of
head-on anger he had displayed in the canteen was
healthy. Indeed before the tea break was over he felt he
had achieved quite another standing with the younger
men. Smithy had offered his hand, returning the diary.
Danny the firebrand. With a little effort he might even
become their spokesman, get management to put the
numbers back on the telephones, achieve something tan-
gible that would improve conditions. It was as if the
whole plane of his concern had shifted from the personal

to the social, his sullen longing for some unattainable truth within himself transformed within minutes into the kind of anger the world understood. He might strike out again in future but it would be for other reasons, loud plausible ones, and Dympna would be proud of him. But would he ever again swing a chair at what had been for one brilliant moment the real and mighty enemy that was yet as elusive as the air, the face one glimpsed in a crowd, in a bit of depersonalised plastic, that was one's own pitted against gratitude for what was less than life, scarcely more than insult?

The candle flame rose tall and sleek, flattened. He thought of a long black wave ever-breaking with a few bright blue flecks of phosphorescence. On the ceiling his head and shoulders hulked ten feet tall. He closed a huge hand over the light flex and it slid down and away, moving nothing. The house shook as another lorry thundered past. When the noise had faded a cry was heard, a sharp angry aaah! that died on the air yet echoed in the minds of people sitting in their shadowy rooms. A fight somewhere in the small warren of redbrick houses? They waited for the shouts, the breaking glass, but there was nothing.

The bedroom door opened and Danny's mother looked in. Danny stood with his back to her, holding his wrist.

'Did you call, Danny?' she said.

'No.'

'Dympna is below.'

When he said nothing she approached and took his hand in hers, turning it over. The skin across the palm was taut and shiny, a rising silver weal that caught the gentle candlelight.

'Jesus, child,' she said after a moment's wonder, 'what have you done to yourself? Water, come on, quick, into water with it!'

Excerpts from the Journal of a Confirmed Bachelor

September 14. At cousin Sibyl's for tea. Gus not there, probably off in a sulk. Atmosphere in the house more and more strained. An effort to sit in the kitchen with Sibyl. Kids disappeared. I have to restrain the urge to grab a brush and clean the place. Bluebottles. I rarely see Gus in the kitchen and I wouldn't blame him. Chilly and Sibyl slips on her old dressing gown that smells of sweat and burnt cork. She seems to live in it. It's obvious that Gus brings out the streel in her and she provokes the pedant in him.

She was playing the intellectual misfit as usual, squashing out one fag after another in the cold tea bags. I recalled Gus as a student lecturing me as we strolled down the Mardyke about the French family, the long leisurely allsharing meals. Tragique. And I remembered what fine stews and things she could make. I put my foot in it at once by telling her not to worry about what she's *really* suited for but to take any job and see where it leads, get out of the house. She nearly spat at me: *any job, out of the house*. Occupational therapy for the bored housewife. I said I didn't say that. No, she said, but you meant it. Then on to Gus again. Apparently he has now advanced to using three cloths and towels for his various zones. What can I say? What I would like to say is that if *she* washed consistently for a while and *he* didn't, the marriage might be saved. But everything is fought out as usual in the area of personality. He has become an automaton. Then: had I listened to his stomach? Not intently, no, I said. It talks, she said. 'Quite seriously, Bill, it tries to tell me things, *real* things.' By nine I was badly in need of a *real* pint.

September 19. A few pints with Gus in Dorans. After about the third he tells me that Sibyl is suffering from 'congenital lack of political will.' On the mother's side. Did I remember the mother? Yes, yes, he interrupts me, a marvellous woman altogether. I know exactly what you're going to say: tall and gracious, cultured, drifting around like a character in a Vir. Woolfe novel, but indolent, essentially parasitical. Our servants will bring us out our tea. He wasn't suggesting that Sibyl wanted servants but mentally she was walking about some terrace having brilliant conversations with people. Did I know Gussy Jr. wanted to study computers? Well if Sibyl had her way he'd be hanging about the house all day hair-splitting about Life. She'd turn him into a 'wet.' Gussy Jr. isn't a wet, I said. I have to say something. Of course not, says Gus, the boy has brains, you only have to look at him. Which is true. Gussy Jr.'s forehead seems to run right around his head. Then farce: my ear must have gradually inclined towards his midriff because he says to me, 'What are you listening to?' Luckily I thought of his old fob. I thought it was giving a funny tick, I said (as if I could hear!). The only funny tick around, says he, is Sibyl.

September 25. Passed Gus on O'Connell Street. Parasitical, he shouted at me. I nodded at him, pretending he was a madman. People looking after him.

October 5. Special command from Sibyl to come out for

Sunday tea again. Can't really refuse unless I'm away as 'confirmed bachelor' etc.

Watched boring television, everyone monosyllabic. Sultry atmosphere as before a storm. Gussy Jr. picks his nose as if he expects to find gold in it. Mary writing an essay on the Common Market. The storm broke. Mind pap, said Sibyl, switching off the set. Then she goes on to talk about Dublin in the old days and how she'd like to have been a hostess somewhere spreading 'slander and truth.' She said she'd like to be really evil for a change instead of pretending to be good. Nice talk, said Gus, with her children listening. She should cop herself on, she was an ordinary Christian woman and shouldn't be going around saying she wanted to be evil, acting what she wasn't. What was she acting? The intellectual slut, he said. Coming it a bit heavy even from Gus with his righteous blood up. I pick up one of Gus's mother's free range eggs from a basket beside me and hand it to Sibyl. As a joke. No joke to her. Down she scrunches it on Gus's sandy mop. Fair as ever, I hand one to Gus. Laurel and Hardy stuff. Sibyl waits and though I thought he'd chicken out, down it came on her gypsy locks. For a moment real catharsis in the air. I should have smashed a few myself, taken their hands, danced around. But poor Gus gives a kind of sob and stumbles out of the room. Sibyl shrugging as if this happens every Sunday, wanders into the back kitchen and puts her head under the tap. Gussy Jr., like the good boy he is, cleans up. Mary at table looking pale and contemplative, perhaps considering career in the convent. Moi, I get the hell away.

October 6. Where are my sympathies? I can believe that Sibyl is indeed looking for some 'real' response, something she feels has been denied her in life. Tired of platitudes she takes it out on Gus. What I hold against her is that she doesn't accept that Gus is in fact a devout conventional man. She wants *him* to act what he isn't. Whereas I feel all she need do is change her attitude. But catch me saying that to Sibyl—not with the breadknife handy.

October 17. Gus seeks me out in Doheny's. I'm becoming confessor to both and really want to hand in the job. I have never wanted to pierce the mystery of marriage and do not intend to. Gus tells me he has asked Sibyl to come along with him to the charismatics! He should have his head examined. Sibyl joining hands and shouting hosannas? Of course stranger things happen and there's always the road to Dundrum but . . . Naturally she refuses but tells him (she is cruel) that such an 'ordered, almost ritualised release of emotion' would be just up his street. Am I that bad? he says and my heart goes out to him. He really means well and has more natural goodness than any man I know. Do you mean to tell me, I said, that your ovidextrous counterattack last Sunday week was merely an ordered ritualised release of egg yoke? And he beamed. Like a little boy he had been waiting for the plaudits. That's what the family needs, I told him, some *real* action. Sure we can't go around chucking eggs at each other, he said, looking shocked. No, but be more spontaneous, I urged. Come home with your shirt tails out and a song on your lips. Escapism, Bill, he said. No, drink wasn't his way at all. Two hours later we were out in Roundwood playing darts and still discussing whether it was his way. Flowers, he said, on the way home. We must have flowers. We must have pulled down half a hedge and filled the car. Don't you think Sibyl is a fine woman when she's dressed up? he said. Very fine features, I said. Stark. Lives up to her name. Stark, he repeated. That's the word, bloody stark. Then we ran over a rabbit and nothing would do Gus but we should take him home as well. He spread the evening paper on his lap and cradled the poor thing, crooned to it. Then he said, you're my best friend, and I thought he was talking to the old rabbit but a hand appeared out of the foliage and shook me till I nearly drove into the ditch I was laughing so much. 'S true, Bill, he said, different an' all as we are. We launched into The Banks, which I find I only do now on such gory occasions.

October 20. Doheny's. The snug. A crowd of us crammed in and Gus appears. He's beginning to look puffy around the eyes and if he didn't squint I would have thought he was starting one. How did it go? All right, he said. That was an awful lot of vegetation. The way he said it I had a picture of what happened and I nearly laughed. He had found enough vases and things? Just about, he said. He didn't wake anyone? He looked surprised. At two in the morning? The only trouble was the rabbit. What did he do with it? Well, he skinned it in the bathroom and cleaned it and hung it up by clothes pegs on the line over the bath. After which he flopped down on the sofa and fell fast asleep. During the night the rabbit drops out of its pegs and into the bath. Enter Mary next morning for her ablutions. Mary screams. Bath looks like someone has been rehearsing in it for Psycho. Sibyl appears, takes one look and returns to bedroom. Gus slinks off to work.

October 22. Thought: in marriage people stalk the elemental in each other. Facades that are accepted in outsiders are hated and pulled down. Sibyl seems determined to storm the walls of Gus's bastion. Dangerous? For me, a shoddy humanist, the elemental in Gus has the whiff of scorched earth. When a man of his conviction loses his sense of goodness, evil is apt to march in like a smiling thug and take over the town. And rape and murder Sibyl into the bargain. But I'm determined to keep out of it.

October 28. Meet Gus by chance in Daly's bar. Standing

there alone like a drifter. Does he go home at all now after work? We are silent with each other, sipping our beer. Tell-tale signs of physical neglect that unnerve me—a dirty hanky, black thumbnail, unpolished shoes. Like finding evidence of rank growth in a proudly tended garden. Spots of dried blood on his ear lobes. Another fracas in which Sibyl impressed more than the points of her argument? I didn't want to ask. I wondered vaguely if he was down to two, even one, body cloth and if this was the whole object of Sibyl's campaign, the arousal of sensual rather than hygienic man.

She was applying other methods too. He starts telling me about 'this guy Joe' who's ringing Sibyl up at all hours. One of the 'wets' from the Arts Club. Shaking his head and smiling. Then a vulgar jibe at the Pope all the more shocking coming from Gus. The Pope in Rome was telling us not to regard our wives as sex objects—well, the poor man needn't trouble his head, a bloody punch-bag would be more like it. He tells me that he has begun to thump Sibyl in his dreams—but actually does it—and in her mysterious way she accepts it, never complains (perhaps believing that in this way too, like his stomach talking, he is trying to convey something 'real'). That they still sleep together is amazing. I'd demand danger money.

October 29. Have decided to spend Christmas in Paris with D. If the parents can be squared.

November 7. Higgens leaving. Big carouse. By ten sing-song in full swing in Burke's back room. Old Foley there with his wife, a devoted pair. Why isn't May Foley my second cousin? She reminds me of my mother, even the way she tells a story. Perhaps it was that or that they were all settled couples and I was feeling very much the confirmed bachelor or imagining poor Gus sitting somewhere brooding by himself but all at once I'm filled with this great rage towards Sibyl. A right battle heat. Remember thinking if I was Cuchulain my right eye would be like a boil on my neck. Off I go to phone and tell her what an old bitch she is and couldn't she show a gramme of plain human warmth for a decent Corkman.

Hello, she says, and whatever got into me (and well I know, I was twisted as a root) I put on this high dainty tone and in my best Montenotte say, Helleo, could I speak to Mr. Dean please. One moment, she says, and then Gus comes on. It's me, Angela, I said. Angela? He sounded as if he had just woken up. And I go into this fierce whisper telling him to keep his voice down and to be mad at me for ringing him at home. The poor man thought he had a nut case on the line but then he twigged and gave an odd kind of giggle. Angela! he cried, how nice! Be angry, I said. Oh I couldn't be angry with you, Angela, he said, you're my life. I suddenly realised that if I was twisted, Gus was knotted entirely. Oh passion, said he, and I hung up.

November 20. Dodged Gus on Grafton Street. He seemed in a hurry, coat tails flying. The sadness of it. Here we are, friends from our youth, having sorted out the world's problems even before we left college, and now dodging each other on the street (correction: I doubt if Gus would try to dodge me—so is he still the only honest one?).

November 27. Sibyl appeared in a dream as a witch. You must wash your dressing gown three times every morning, she cackled. When I refused she chased me all around the Wicklow hills.

December 5. Sibyl rang. What would I like for Christmas? Money, I said, as much as you can spare. Slowly we got around to the reason for her calling. Was I attending a philosophy course too? Philosophy course? Gus apparently was into philosophy. Bully for him, I said. She seemed to find the idea ridiculous—as if all he should ever read was his E.S.B. accounts! I told her I'd give her a pair of eye-openers for Christmas. Nasty man, she said, and hung up.

December 8. Occurs to me that Sibyl must think there's a terrible bitchy streak in me.

December 19. Deposited my few presents on Deans' doorway as if I was pinching the milk. Thought I glimpsed Sibyl behind the curtains. All the way to town saw her lips curling in a smile. Just the kind of behaviour she feeds on. Paris, cleanse me with your rough brazen (expensive!) passions!

January 7. Wondering what's become of Gus—we didn't even have a New Year drink—when phone rings just as I'm going out. Sibyl. Hello, she says, very grand, this is Angela. All right, I said, *mea culpa*. I had a picture of her sitting in her old dressing gown unchanged down to the last tea bag. Tell me, she says, after we had exchanged tepid New Year greetings, how's Gloria? Gloria? Gus's Gloria, she says, G-G, didn't I think it sounded like a vaudeville act? You're joking, I said. The old neocortex was doing a jig. Divil a joke, boy, says she, in a Cork accent. Gloria was *quite* convincing on the phone. Well, Sibyl, I said, it only balances things out, don't you think? How's Joe these days? Do Corkmen tell each other everything? she asked sweetly. (It only occurred to me then that all her life she may have had it in for Corkmen or the Cork accent). Then she said, it's not the morality of it I'm worried about, Bill, as I'm sure you'll appreciate. I just don't want Gus to make a fool of himself, I owe him *that* much. And she hung up. I can't wait to phone him.

January 8. He sounded quite pleased that I had rung and a bit formal. A drink? Certainly, old man. Usual place? He arrived sporting a blond moustache that made him look like Dr. Watson. Since when the tash? says I. Do you like it? he said, touching it with a perfectly manicured nail. Hygienic man was well in command again. I figured he must be up to at least four body cloths. He had new kid gloves and wore a light beige poloneck instead of the waistcoat. He was strangely naked without the fob. We sipped our drinks and then I said, impish like, how's Gloria? Oh you've been talking to the Sibyl, have you? Oracles galore, I said. Tell, tell. Nothing much to tell really, he said. Gloria and I are good friends. Oh really? Amicable, he said. Platonic like, says I. Warm, says he. Ah, says I, completely at sea. And he shut up like a clam. For half an hour we chatted politely but the effort was great. He fidgeted a lot and it was only when he was about to leave that I said we should have a drink sometime, *a trois*. Fine, he said. He sounded as if he didn't care one way or the other. We have arranged to meet at M's on Bachelor's Walk on Monday evening.

January 12. Turning into Bach. Walk I'm overcome by sense of unreality. Meeting Gus and lady friend? As if I'm being invited to some weird ceremony of laicisation. But reality immediately less daunting. Gloria is about thirty-five with thin flaxen hair and soft regular features and, as far as I could judge, a rather soft irregular body. Very little waist but quite a lot of arm and thigh. (At least when at one point her arm snaked past me for the salt I was astonished at its range.) Motherly was the word that immediately sprang to mind—in her manner of talking as well though she may have been putting it on as a kind of valve. Our immediate valve was wine. We must have got through the first bottle in five minutes flat.

Where had they met? In Dwyers in the lunch break. I found it rather touching, two lonely people having their toasted sandwiches and striking up a conversation. They had always sat in the same corner of the bar. And the fact, said Gloria, that they were both into the occult meant that they immediately had something in common. I glanced at Gus with a kind of silly grin which he reciprocated. It was like learning that St. Thomas consulted the ouija board when he wasn't writing the Summa. Then he tried to look dignified but his nose was running. She handed him tissues. That's what he wanted, someone to mother him. But I still wondered if the relationship was quite that chaste. And *that's* what cousin Sibyl would want to know of course.

While Gus was in the gents Gloria hinted that Gus was going through a crisis of faith and she was trying to help him. She herself had made the transition from Catholicism fairly easily but it must be traumatic for a man like Gus whose faith had been so firm—and still was, she added, in many ways (which probably meant that it *was* chaste, he was doing the great balancing act and enjoying the mothering in the meantime). And of course, she said, his wife being so rigidly Catholic didn't help. I was just taking a sip of wine and she had to slap me on the back to prevent me from choking on it.

Dawned on me then that far from Gus simply wanting the companionship of a motherly woman the whole scene was part of an elaborate joke. This must have been written all over me because when Gus returned to the table his grin was bolder, a smirk almost. And the smirk broadened when to my dismay I realised that for some time Gloria had been openly flirting with me (I was a far better proposition surely), tapping the hand, once quite significantly pressing the knee, telling me she knew what scoundrels these confirmed bachelors were, and here we were on Bachelor's Walk, wasn't it a scream, though she didn't believe it of me. I had a kind of intellectual face but I seemed very tense. Would I like to go along with her to the Theosophical Group some evening? I'd be amazed what peace entered my soul when I was truly opened to the Oneness of life . . . Gus was grinning broadly now and I thought of my silly phone call and all the other little ways I had unwittingly exposed him to ridicule. He was having his fun which was also his revenge, on Sibyl and myself.

Twelve o'clock! Worst fears of persecution confirmed: Gloria on the phone just now hoping I didn't mind ringing so late (had she asked Gus for my number, did he *offer* it, the sneaky hoor?) but she just had to call and tell me how much she appreciated all that I had done and was doing for Gus as a friend. She would definitely drop over that book she had on the Lifetide. Drop it over!!! No trouble at all, says she We could have a nice chat together.

NNB. Ring Gus tomorrow *to call her off*. A joke's a joke.

January 13. Eleven o'clock rang Gus. He hadn't reported for work. Rang home. Gussy Jr. on the line sounding breathless. Apparently Daddy had stayed in bed with his cold but then Mammy had fallen off a ladder (a ladder?) and fractured her wrist or something and Daddy had to get up and drive her to the hospital but on the way they had an accident and now they were both in hospital.

Off I go at lunchtime to the hospital and there stood this fine tall garda. I told him I was a friend of Mr. Dean and he nodded and even smiled upon me as if he thoroughly approved. Then he told me that Gus was in the way of becoming Ireland's numero uno hero for foiling the getaway of bank robbers. Apparently on the way to the hospital they were just coming up to a bank when these bandits came running out with masks and shotguns and all the rest. What does Gus do (I'd swear he'd been having a nice argument with Sibyl) but head straight for them, ramming their car and causing one of them to discharge his shotgun through the windscreen. But Gus and Sibyl had ducked and Gus only got a few pellets in the arm. Not only that (according to a witness who had come in the car with them) the robbers managed to get their car going and were swinging around when Gus rammed them *again* shouting like a madman, and even when the robbers were running away he was backing up like a 'dotty puck goat' for yet another ram at a totally empty car when he fainted into the arms of his wife.

Knew Gloria would ring. Lucky twice when I answered. Third time it was her. What could I do but tell her about it. She sounded genuinely distressed. That made two of us.

January 14. Arrive at the hospital when place is full of press photographers. They had wheeled the two beds together in a room so that the whole family could pose, Gussy Jr. and Mary too. From some feeling of admiration (and awe) my mood darkening quickly into pique, especially when Sibyl ropes me into a photo as her cousin. Razmataz, and she was loving every moment of it. Her arm was broken in three places, several ribs broken. Gus really had himself a ball. I heard her tell one of the reporters that they might get away from it all for a while in Tenerife. Just her kind of scene: ambivalence, duplicity, public heroism stemming (as I suspect) from a family row, all mixed up with the hole and corner erotic pranks of the middle class.

And Gus. Apparently one of his eyes had suffered so he'll probably collect a bundle from some judge. At the very least take over the E.S.B. Take good care of G-G while he's in hospital, says Sibyl to me with a sly wink. A right daisy. Gus lay propped up swathed in bandages, his one eye glittering with triumph. Catharsis? You could have put a ribbon on it. And I could see the whole codology of it, the two of them holding hands like a couple of romantic refugees from East Germany who had made it in a balloon. Just ye wait, I wanted to shout, it'll soon be back to the bluebottles and tea bags!

Walking down the long hospital corridor I wondered if it would. A tall gaunt priest passed me and smiled, a man of about my own age. I glanced after him, treading as if afraid of slipping on the shiny corridor, and I thought how knowing I was, perched like a cocky bird on the gargoyle of some doomed church, untouched for all my concern by the anguish in the stone, by hope, its wild guttering and death.

Salvage Operation

The covers were thrown back as if she had only intended to air them. Antonio's dark blue pyjamas lay neatly folded on the pillow but he would have done that. According to Alice he made 'quite deliberate' concessions to sexual equality. Perhaps folding his own pyjamas was one. The pillows still held the imprint of their heads and Allan, standing at the foot of the bed, wondered how she had behaved the night before, the last night. Had she wanted to make love and, if so, why? To lull Antonio into a sense of their continuing life together, to celebrate (but surely with little joy) its termination?

A few hair clips, cotton wool pads, were strewn on the dressing table. Beside it the piano stool lay on its side. Righting it, Allan found when he sat down that his eyes were above the level of the mirror and this, rather than the visual memory of Alice sitting there, evoked the feel and shape of her body. Gangly was a word that came to him when he first saw it, the limbs curiously loose and disjointed. She had turned there at the wardrobe as if to present her nakedness to his eye before submitting to his touch, and perhaps it was her manner of doing so that suggested the word, shyly, as if she were a thin gawky-looking athlete anxious to prove that in motion all would be grace and harmony. But their love-making had been rough, shameless. Going home to Fran was to return, he had often felt, from a scratching cat of a girl to the pliant shock-absorbing flesh of woman. Yet both were the same age. In the end the scratches on his back gave the game away.

He noticed too that the angle of the mirror reflected (intentionally?) the one in the hall and that in turn caught the back of Fran's head where she sat in the front room nervously thumbing the underside of her ring finger. What a bizarre ending the whole affair was taking. It was as if they had returned to the scene of a crime now expiated but echoing still in the abandoned rooms, in soft piano music coming from somewhere, the faintly prurient odours of the dressing table, the dark forbidding stroke of the grandfather clock. It seemed, too, such an age ago though he (bending slightly towards the mirror) had hardly changed in the few intervening years. Their passage had given it the finished quality of an act in a play. At the time he had indeed anticipated some sound literary return for the generous investment of his passion. He had craved 'experience'. And the situation had promised all kinds of significant goodies: two disaffected people, she with a husband who wanted her on a pedestal which she was determined to hack to bits; he with a wife who had gone strange on him after the death of their first baby. Fran had turned to the spirit in a way that alienated him. He hadn't believed in it, thought of it as sneaking guiltily and under reprimand through a side gate back into the Garden. But when he hinted at this, gently at first, arguing that *he* certainly didn't feel any divine reprimand, Fran had only withdrawn further. While not denying herself to him, her sexual disinterest was palpable. Infidelity had gratefully donned its own moral garb. When one day, conscience-struck, he had more vehemently challenged the inscrutable Will she had cried, 'You can't taunt Him, ever. So don't taunt me!'

Allan had seen his own situation reflected in Alice's rejection of her husband's demands for conformity to a feminine ideal. She had, as she put it, to 'represent' woman rather than be one. The religious difference seemed hardly to matter though Alice had been shocked to discover, on her first visit to Antonio's small town in Spain, that his mother had been going around telling the neighbours that she was Catholic but an 'American Catholic,' whatever that was. 'Talk about the moral community in Ireland,' she had laughed. 'Converted in absentia!' Physical attraction—on the crest of which she had married him—she found was neatly locked away in a compartment of Antonio's mind. When not indulging it in the marriage bed (significantly, according to Alice at the time, he disliked making love anywhere else) she was expected, albeit in the most 'progressive' manner and particularly so since the birth of a son, to aspire to the nobler ideals, social and maternal. This was more subtle than the conventional and much-maligned having to be there with the food on the table and a vigorous 'Hello, darling!' on the tongue—that, after all, could be treated, or mistreated, as 'normal'. She was expected to perform with a certain style. 'Doña bloody hostess,' she had complained, spreadlegged on the carpet. In fact from initially seeing Antonio as burdened by the familiar patriarchal bias of his race, Alice had come to the belief that it was nothing more hereditary than the snob, even the would-be aristocrat, rising above his lowly origins.

How smugly, Allan reflected, elongating a smear of cream on the table, they had been able here in this bedroom to demarcate self and spouse, to cast outline and character as in brilliant holograms into the air around. Yet they were just that, mere images as frail and insecure as any thrown on a spotty screen. Fran had proved that at once. One night when the affair was at its height — Antonio was conveniently away on business — Allan emerged from the house to find Fran waiting for him in the car.

'Had a good poker game?' she said. 'Lose much?'

Before he could reply she was getting out, slamming the door and striding towards the house. Allan lit an upside-down cigarette that nearly choked him. The situation had taken a somewhat too dramatic turn for his literary soul. But a strange thing happened. The door opened. Fran was admitted by Alice in her dressing gown. The door closed. Allan waited for the shrill of voices. Nothing. Silence but for an occasional car. Minutes passed. Lights went out along the street. The city was settling down to its hard-earned rest. What on earth were they saying to each other?

Later, when he tried to worm it out of them, each in turn, he was annoyed to discover that they had been sitting in the kitchen where he could easily have eavesdropped (as after a quarter of an hour he had been tempted to do) and not in the front room. They had talked, they said, just talked. However, from a word that Alice used to the effect that Fran had been 'loving' towards her from the start, the conclusion was inescapable that Fran's hope (though hardly articulate) on approaching the house had been to claim in a spirit of forgiveness not only her husband but the friendship of the woman with whom he had betrayed her. Perhaps Alice was simply overawed, seeing in Fran's bearing and attitude the Brave New Woman. But if story there were, Allan had thought, then this was it. In a spirit of wonder it would go on to trace not the gradual collapse of Alice's marriage and the halting recovery of their own but the forging of a deep friendship between two such different women. Nor was it a question of Fran bringing missionary zeal to bear (though she tried her damndest to save the marriage) on the hedonist—Alice continued to have her lovers, once even 'babysitting' in their home with one of them, a young man she had met at an extramural course (Allan: 'Ha, ha, very good,' shaking his hand)—it was that *he*, randy Al, was no longer one of them while *they* (and now the word was Fran's, linking Alice along a beach in Kerry) had become 'sisters'.

And more: each in her own fashion, Alice flirtatiously and ironically, Fran strongly and silently allowing him vast freedom to do as he pleased, had engendered in him a sense of guilt as if he alone were the culprit. For weeks he had coldly exploited that freedom, avoiding the company of females as one would a nest of wiles, drinking too much, and then discovering through a friend the world of the genuine punter and writing about it. The price was high. He lost money. Endless poker games in a school of Corkmen as smooth and hard as the Blarney stone sapped his energies. Fran's father was obliged to pay one debt. He was weak, they said, unreliable, implying she should never have married him. But then after one night of tenderness and talk their marriage had begun again and soon afterwards Fran had conceived Lilly . . .

Allan realised that the low music he had thought was just audible from next door was in fact coming from the bedside radio. He switched it off, catching, as he bent, a hint of Alice's perfume. The first day he had called (with a translation for Antonio's firm) she was pacing about, dabbing herself with it as if to ward off an evil. 'Do you like it?' she had asked suddenly, exposing her neck to him. 'Extract of Burren flowers no less, a present from my adoring husband.' He had breathed in its fragrance and she had remained close to him, offering him, as though in animal submission, her throat. But when he had tried to kiss it (himself quite eager to submit) she had darted away with a laugh.

Going towards the bedroom door he spotted the other red slipper peeping from beneath the curtain. Its fellow, perched on a kitchen chair, had bothered him. It must have bothered Alice too as she rushed about packing, fleeing. Would they fit Fran?

'They're late,' she said when he entered the room. She meant the furniture removers. They were 'salvaging' Alice's cherished pieces before Antonio returned. She was fleeing finally, irrevocably, defying his present refusal to separate—there had been one trial separation—or even to allow her to travel home alone with little Partick. Once back in the States he knew she would not return. What added dramatic spice to the situation was his cancellation at the last minute of a business trip. 'As if he knew,' Alice had said, grimly. But she was resolute. The ticket had been paid for, the salvaging operation arranged, she was going.

'On the dot of eleven, the silly man said,' Fran complained. 'He even repeated it. You heard him. "On the dot, madam." '

'We are living in a country, my dear,' said Allan in a poetic voice, 'where the dimensions of time are not those of ordinary mortals. They are closer to those celestial realms where time. . .'

'Would you mind?'

'I've found it,' he said showing her the pair of slippers. 'Would they fit you?'

'I wouldn't wear them.'

'Afraid Antonio would drop in and see them? Might as well be killed for a slipper as a grandfather clock.'

'I'm not afraid of Antonio.'

'Certainly you're not. You even went to the theatre with him, an amazing feat of endurance.' He blew a speck from the toe of one slipper. 'What was it you wanted to do with him? Unbend his brooding gaucho soul? No, something much simpler. You had wanted him to laugh, just once, heartily, unmistakeably humanly. To win Alice back with laughter. But what was the good when Alice wasn't there to hear him? It was like laughing in the desert. What still amazes me is that he loves her—and, mark my words, he'll get her back yet and on *his* terms.'

'I doubt it very much.'

'Try them on.'

'I don't *want* to,' Fran said, fiercely. 'I want nothing.' He turned to begin his pacing again when she added, 'Except that picture.'

Allan glanced at it and recalled that it used to hang in the bright hallway. At what bitter moment was it banished to the dark alcove beside the chimney breast? Was that why Fran wanted it, to rescue it back into the light as a testimony to what had been? 'What is is,' she had repeated as in a prayer when the baby died. 'What is' was the Will. And was Alice proving that what was needn't be?

A smiling Alice approached along a path in a park. Looking closer Allan saw that Lilly was the baby on the grass beside a strange pram. To the rear Antonio, a spare looking intense man, was bending to guide his toddling son. Was it because of Lilly that she . . . ? Turning with the question on his lips it died in the lacklustre of her gaze, the sad feasting on what was lost.

He stood observing her as though she were inanimate, a figure in an interior, jacket firmly moulded to waist and hip, tilt of auburn head, full slightly uneven breasts, a button in her blouse cunningly undone—but as if he too were looking past her (as she would unconsciously feel) into a wastage of time and love, a pool where things waved and broke as in a dream. For a while neither moved. Baby Joe in his carrycot sighed, and a sentence formed: *This is how they would find us overcome by fumes and ash, this long petrified moment of recall.*

Recall? He waited for a movement and it came, the habitual nervous thumbing of the ring finger. Held by it, what he suddenly recalled was their first Christmas in his home, the sharp clear breath of hunger after midnight Mass, across the fields the beacon of the house with fires built up and golden, plump puddings hooked along the kitchen ceiling, the glinting hoop of the road binding it all, holding their world together in the frosty air—and where their bodies, lured in thought, the bed, waiting in its pale of starlight, unearthly, it appeared on entering the room, repellant, until fingers whisked across the curtains and the table lamp flung its familiar arch over the warm red walls . . .

Fran was observing him now and their eyes met, faltered, and as he began to pace again the scene burst, became a joke in a cracker, a treasure trove spat upon by clowns. Its place filled with the memory of a row much later when he had wanted a sherry before lunch, Fran at the fire smiling to herself and not taking his part, while his mother lectured him on the evils of drink. A lousy sherry! 'But that's how it starts, boyeen.' Benighted, puritanical peasants! He had spent the day cold and sulking on the river bank.

He replaced the slippers on the kitchen chair as if this were now part of an irresistible order. The grandfather clock struck the half hour. Allan checked with his watch. Twelve o'clock flight to New York. Alice would be sitting watching the television screen, responding mechanically to Patrick's chatter. Perhaps like a rogue thought the whereabouts of the other slipper taunted her.

Pacing back into the hall his head droned as if he were suffering from hangover. From the doorway he eyed the brandy bottle on the sideboard, noted again the tilt of Fran's head as if to gauge her mood. Light slanting in, woman, cot, amber bottle, made a piece set for the brush of a Dutch master. Under his tread a board creaked and Fran said, 'Must you?'

'What?'

'Pace.'

He ignored her, stepped carefully between the lines and stars on the carpet, thought of a recent walk over Sandymount strand. Mounds of dark heavy sand thrown

up by the worm diggers. Sea graves looted of their treasure. He stood among them, bent occasionally to throw a
worm into the bucket, felt at peace. The wind tugged him
like an impatient child towards the sea and he strode out
as if leaving the city for good on foot. Gulls angled in the
last rays of the sunlight and pink and tender as in a
Japanese print. The moon filled the horizon with its
ghostly sail. But when he turned again on the wrinkling
sands back towards the lights, the darkening mass of
land, the birds were black and bat-like, as suddenly as
were his thoughts of change that remained pretty phrases,
poetry rising like bile.

> *My thoughts print a path*
> *to the waves. In a flash I*
> *turn trampling them out.*

Growth. What a stirring illusion! One believed in it,
toadied to words to make it real. The city's humdrum
entered him again like a slow familiar poison . . .

'You'll get something out of it eventually, won't you?'
Fran said, quietly.

'What?' He looked at her in surprise.

'This.'

'What's this?'

'The drama and so on.' Flutter of hands signalled her
mood. 'That's why you came along today, isn't it? Not
really to help. Something might go wrong. The fog
mightn't lift, Antonio might come home unexpectedly.
You would have to be *in* on it, the scene, but for what it
could mean to *you*. Damn the fact that Alice . . .' She
choked on the thought, shook her head as if to rid herself
of it. 'Everything is a pawn to you, Allan, isn't it? People,
reality, everything. Everything can be exchanged for a
better card . . . and then despite all the great intellectu-
alising your mind seems to work in such *small* ways. Alice
fleeing into God knows what kind of future and you pace
about   being   intellectual . . . I   know   you,   head

down . . . and then asking me if her slippers would fit. Scavenger.' This last was said in a contemptuous whisper and Allan was stung by it because, though he had stood disarmed by her tirade, by its truth that echoed his own thoughts as he paced about the room, his suggestion that she should try on the slippers was made in the spirit of Alice's urging them to take anything she left behind. And what, he wondered, were they doing for Alice if not scavenging?

'She said you could take anything . . .'

'I know what she said.'

'And as for fleeing into some terrible future . . . From what I know of her rich Mama, who has always disapproved of that dago Antonio, I very much doubt it.' He reached for the brandy. 'Who's scavenging, will you tell me? Please could you salvage my grandfather clock and my Regency bureau and put them into storage? Mama will send for them when the divorce comes through . . .' He took a swig from the bottle, shuddering as the liquor coursed through his gullet. Fran had turned away, as if in disgust, staring at the ground. Swinging the brandy bottle, Allan paced again, stepping on the creaking board.

Scavenger!

'We all scavenge constantly on each other, madam, he rejoined, pacing with haughty, measured tread back into the kitchen.'

The 'drama' of which Fran had spoken was mere movement. Flight, upheaval, were sterile in themselves. What could he hope to have experienced? It was when Alice stood again, as he stood now with his finger on the greasy rim of the cooker, that life began, ended. The rest was a hurried change of scenery and they were outside it, Alice too. It was being done for her by airline pilots and furniture removers and friends who waited to let them in. It could be thrown away in an opening paragraph: *One day Alice fled to America from her possessive, idolising husband. A friendly couple supervised the removal of a few articles she had*

bought with her own money and to which she had grown attached.
Comforted by an understanding mother a new life began for
her . . .

Another scenario, closer to farce, unfolded and he
yielded to it with the same sense of defiance that had
prompted him to reach for the brandy. What if Alice had
to return and the furniture were gone? Would there be a
mad scramble to get it out of storage again before Antonio
returned, perhaps hiring a van which he, Allan, would
have to drive like a madman through the streets of
Dublin . . . ?

When he returned to the room Fran was feeding Joe.
He stood over them, watching or rather hearing the
baby's greedy yng-yng-yng-yng as he burrowed into the
breast.

'Yng-yng-yng.yng,' he said. 'I think he's a milkaholic.
I think perhaps my mother should be consulted. What
do you say?' Fran said nothing, averting her face as from
his brandy breath. *'You're in love with Antonio,' he snarled.*
'You want to be idolised. Admit it, you hussy!'

'No, Allan, I love only you!'

'Liar! All this is a plot to get Alice out of the way. I'll give you
drama!'

'No, Allan, not in front of the child!'

'Yes, he must learn the naked truth.' A button in her blouse was
undone. His passion flared and his cruel fingers ripped at the
fabric . . .

The grandfather clock struck. Twelve deep solemn
notes.

Told you so . . . told you so . . . told you so . . . told you
so . . .

Take-off time. And the fog had lifted, as the radio said
it would. In the hallway Allan stood and looked back into
the room but now the light was matt and coarse. Fran's
hair had lost its sheen, her body its smooth rounded line.
She slumped squat and imageless in the chair. She was

weeping and he felt nothing. She was right, he was outside grief, waited to barter it as he would a dud card. In her it remained locked up like stubborn phlegm. He thought of two women so different that their friendship had been a kind of exploration. His images of them were of movement and stasis. Alice moved, impatient on the slow drip of life, a ballerina, but one on whose face when she danced close by in the garish light one caught a sluttish smile as if she had seen through the pretence of all creation. And Fran so passive at times, so full of bloodless wisdom, that it maddened him, causing him once to shout, 'Why aren't you more interested in *ideas?*' Yet slowly, almost covertly, as if his limbs resisted the steps, this slow minuet of the heart, he had discovered in her quietude a different awareness of things, different as they were themselves. And he stood by her chair tongue-tied, helpless.

A van drew up in front of the house and with a sense of release Allan bounded to the front door to admit the men. There were two, a young cocky-looking fellow with a carrot top and an older dour individual with spade-like hands. The work was done in a matter of minutes, first the grandfather clock, then the bureau, finally the old Irish settle and carved chest.

When he had given the men a tip and closed the door behind them Allan returned to the room to find Fran fetching glasses from the sideboard and pouring out two brandies. They toasted each other in silence, awkward as if they had never drunk together before in private. The lines of strain were going from her face. She was relieved at least that things had gone well.

On the pavement outside he saw something red under the picture she had wrapped in baby things. The slippers. She caught his glance and smiled.

'I salvaged them after all,' she said, raising her face to him as if she expected him to acknowledge the gesture, perhaps even to kiss her. When he didn't, when he stood indeed looking at her rather sternly as if now she had been weak and irresponsible (he was feeling slightly drunk), she turned to move towards the car. But she halted and faced him again.

'Are there any real stories, Allan?'

Perhaps what we salvage, madam, each alone in his world?

'I don't know.'

They stood by the car as if reluctant to get in, finally to end it. He held up Alice's shiny Yale key. 'What will we do with it?'

Fran took it and held it over the drain in the gutter.

'Don't worry,' she said. 'I'm not going to brood over it all.'

She still held it, looking sideways at him as if to tease him.

She dropped the key. It hit off one of the bars, balanced precariously on the rim.

It dropped cleanly through the bars, landing with a little snick in the dead leaves.